BILL, THE GALACTIC HERO

VOLUME 4

ON THE PLANET OF ZOMBIE VAMPIRES

BILL, THE GALACTIC HERO

VOLUME 4

ON THE PLANET OF ZOMBIE VAMPIRES

HARRY HARRISON

AND JACK C. HALDEMAN II

Artwork by Michael W. Kaluta

A Byron Preiss Book

AVON BOOKS ◆ NEW YORK

BILL, THE GALACTIC HERO ON THE PLANET OF ZOMBIE
VAMPIRES (#4) is an original publication of Avon Books. This work
has never before appeared in book form. This work is a novel. Any
similarity to actual persons or events is purely coincidental.

Special thanks to Nat Sobel, Eleanor Wood, John Douglas, Chris Miller,
David Keller, and John Betancourt.

AVON BOOKS
A division of
The Hearst Corporation
105 Madison Avenue
New York, New York 10016

BILL, THE GALACTIC HERO ON THE PLANET OF ZOMBIE
VAMPIRES copyright © 1991 by Byron Preiss Visual Publications, Inc.
Introduction copyright © 1991 by Harry Harrison
Illustrations copyright © 1991 by Byron Preiss Visual Publications, Inc.
Published by arrangement with Byron Preiss Visual Publications, Inc.
Cover and book design by Alex Jay/Studio J.
Edited by David M. Harris
Front cover painting by Michael Wm. Kaluta and Steven Fastner
Library of Congress Catalog Card Number: 90-93564
ISBN: 0-380-75665-X

First Avon Books Printing: April 1991

For Lori,
a true fan of aliens everywhere,
especially those slimy ones.

In space, no one can hear you dream

CHAPTER 1

BILL KICKED THE BUCKET. THEN HE kicked a chair, reducing it to splinters. It wasn't that he was angry—though he had good reason to be teed-off and touchy. Stuck here on this puny supply station in the middle of nowhere. He, a Galactic Hero, now reduced to the most menial of menial labor. He sniveled self-pityingly at the faded memories of past glories, for he had been reduced to driving a forklift, loading giant boxes of multipurpose paper onto outgoing spacers. It was sandpaper on one side, toilet paper on the other, and woe befall he who did not read the instructions on the box. No, crappy as this job was, his real concern was a physical problem of a most personal nature. His right foot was turning to stone, and he was losing control over it. He sniveled again, stamped with sudden, bitter anger, then pulled his foot out of the hole in the floor.

It had started out as a real nice foot. Bill even got used to all the extra toes, but this turning-to-stone business was getting out of hand. Or rather out of foot. It currently weighed in at thirty-five pounds and was gaining weight fast. Bill felt like he was dragging a cinder block around with him, and once he got it moving it was hard to stop, short of crashing it into something. The crew aboard the supply station gave him plenty of room, and repair robots followed him around like mechanical puppy dogs.

Bill realized that he had a bad habit of losing body parts. The thought depressed him greatly, and he flicked a tear from one moist eye. He had lost what used to be his left arm through no fault of his own while becoming a Galactic Hero. That's what war is all about. That it had been replaced with a right arm, a nice black one that had belonged to a friend of his—it gave Bill something to remember him by—was something he had grown quite used to, even fond of. He was attached to his new arm, and was always inventing new fun things to do with it.

The foot, however, was another matter. Bill had blown his original foot away himself in a flash of self-preservation designed to keep all of his body parts from being even more disastrously blown away in a hopeless battle against the dreaded Chingers.

The official military line was that the crazed Chingers were the cause of almost every horrible thing that had ever happened in the universe. Reptilian in nature and bad to the bone, it was said they stood seven feet tall and ate human babies for breakfast. With Tabasco.

Bill knew better.

Seven inches was more like their physical size, and before the Space Troopers had started blasting them away, the Chingers hadn't even had a word for violence. Although they were peace-loving and friendly, they were not stupid. They were also quick learners. And hated Tabasco. So the Emperor had an intergalactic war to keep his troops busy, and Bill had two right arms, a cinder block for a foot, and an enlistment contract with an automatic extension clause.

This was not the first foot transplant Bill had ever had. All of them had been disastrous. Though maybe not the first one, a giant chicken foot. He had become attached to that foot, and vice versa of course. But while it was handy for scratching in the sand for bugs, it wouldn't fit in his boot and hurt all the time. The fact that his new foot was turning into solid rock probably wasn't anyone's fault. Sometimes bad things just seemed to happen.

Bill kicked open Doctor Hackenslash's door and followed his careening foot into the office.

"You could have knocked, Trooper," squealed the doctor from underneath the desk. "I thought we were under attack."

"No Chinger in its right mind would give this bowby little post a second glance," said Bill, skidding his foot along the floor to stop its momentum. "I've got a more serious problem."

"Possibly your nose this time?" said the doctor hopefully, crawling out from under the desk and brushing chunks of the splintered door off his chair. "Nose problems are my speciality."

Perhaps this was because the good doctor possessed a hooter like an anteater, a great flaring, projecting nose with cavernous nostrils, gloomy hair-filled canyons. He pointed this impressive proboscis at Bill and sniffed.

"You want your nose examined?"

"Only if you have to get to my foot that way. Look at it, doc! It's getting heavier."

"Feet are so boring," sniffed Hackenslash, tapping his own nose with his finger so that it flapped in a most interesting manner. "All those little pink toes wiggling all the time. Give me a nose any day. Deviated septums! Sinus cavities! *Postnasal drip!* Nobody knows the nose better than those who know the nose know."

"My toes aren't pink anymore, and they sure aren't wiggling. They're more like granite. We got to do something."

"How about we wait?" said the doctor, breaking into a sneezing fit on account of all the door dust floating around the room. Bill was knocked back three feet by the force of this nasal blast.

"Wait?" yelled Bill. "I'm dragging a boulder around, and you want to wait?"

"Think of it as a scientific experiment—be brave," said Hackenslash, grabbing a handful of tissue from one of the five boxes on his desk and blowing his nose. Bill cowered under the white blast of shredded Kleenex. "Maybe if we wait it'll spread. Next your knee could turn to stone. Then your whole leg. Maybe even your you-know-what—interesting possibilities there! Perhaps even those two right arms you're so proud of. It might even spread to your *nose*. As a scientist I would be remiss to pass up this opportunity to study such an unusual occurrence."

Bill watched the doctor double over with a seemingly endless attack of the sneezes, and as the physician gobbled up a bunch of antihistamines Bill decided enough was enough. He'd take the hard line.

"As a Trooper with a stone foot I am unfit for battle," said Bill, choking on the word "battle." "As the base doctor it is your sworn and solemn duty to make every soldier in this command shipshape, sturdy, and ready for"—gulp—"warfare. How can I jump into action dragging this boulder around?"

"I like your tusks," said Dr. Hackenslash. "Some elephants have tusks, you know. And nothing beats an elephant when it comes to noses."

The end run from scientific curiosity to flattery didn't work, although Bill was quite fond of his three-inch-long tusks, which he had inherited from the sadistic Deathwish Drang. He felt they gave him a fearsome appearance when he snarled.

"I want a new foot," Bill snarled. "I want to be ready to leap into battle," he lied.

Impressed by the gnashing fangs, the doctor nodded reluctantly.

"As you yourself pointed out, this isn't exactly a sizzling war zone." Dr. Hackenslash pulled out a giant-economy, coffin-sized box of tissue. "Consequently, we have a regrettable lack of replacement parts. In my last assignment we had arms and legs all over the place, boxes of pippicks, bales of ears. But not here. And noses! You should have seen my collection; all kinds, shapes, sizes. I even had one—"

"Wait!" Bill whipped up an especially ferocious snarl. "Does this mean I'm stuck with this rock?"

"Don't do that!" shouted the doctor. "You're making me awfully nervous, and I might botch the surgery. It is quite a delicate procedure. Took years of training."

"So I do get a new foot?"

"In a manner of speaking. Medical supply made a clerical error and sent me eighty-three cases of regenerative foot-buds. I've got thousands of the little suckers, so I suppose I can spare you one. Though I really *would* like to see if your nose turns to stone."

"Let's get with it," growled Bill, tired of dragging the albatross of a stone foot around with him. "Which way's the operating room? Will I have to be prepped? What kind of anesthetic are you going to use? Will it hurt?"

The doctor put a box on the floor and pressed a red button marked WARM UP.

"When the green light comes on, put your foot in the hole on top. I'll give you a hand."

"It's a foot I want!" screamed Bill as the light flashed green and Hackenslash grappled up his foot and dropped it down the hole.

"Just a little professional joke," chuckled the doctor. "We physicians do have a sense of humor beneath our always coolly confident and skillful exteriors."

With exasperating illogic Bill was already getting ready to miss his old foot. The extra toes had been nice. And after it had turned to stone, it had been real handy for propping doors open and kicking things out of his way.

"When will you start the operation?" asked Bill, gritting his teeth in anticipation of the long and involved and certain-to-be-excruciatingly-painful procedure.

"All finished," said Hackenslash proudly. "Take a look."

Bill pulled his foot out of the hole. The first thing he noticed was that he was missing a foot entirely.

"You moron medico!" screamed Bill, waving his stump in the air. "My foot's gone!"

"That's what you wanted, isn't it?"

"But I wanted a replacement, too. What I got now is nothing," he sobbed.

"What you've got is a military grade Mark-1 regenerative foot-bud, Trooper. Take a close look."

Sure enough, there at the end of Bill's stump was a tiny pink bud about the size and shape of a baked bean.

"I did a good job, didn't I—why don't you admit that?" The doctor stood up, bloated with pride, red nose wavering in the air like a giant tomato. "Can I keep your old foot? It'll make a nice paperweight."

Bill was staring at the tiny bud. It still looked like a baked bean.

"Of course, you'll have to stay off that bud until the foot grows out," said Hackenslash, handing him a pair of crutches. "I'm sorry I couldn't make you battle-ready in a jiffy. You'll just have to wait until it grows."

"How long will that take?" smirked Bill gleefully, taking the crutches, which were dented and about twelve sizes too short.

"Quite a long time, I'm afraid. You can't rush mother nature."

"That's really too bad," Bill smarmed insincerely, with visions of weeks of no duty, months of lolling around, years of recuperation. "It pains me not to be able to get back into the fight right away. I guess I'll have to go on permanent sick call."

"That will be up to Commander Cook," said the doctor. "Take this note to him and don't forget to mention that I need a new door."

Bill left Hackenslash's office feeling about thirty-five pounds lighter, and he was halfway to Commander Cook's quarters before his back started killing him from bending over the too-small crutches.

The commander was staring out the window with his hands clasped behind his back when Bill arrived and tried to salute, managing to get all tangled up in his crutches so that he tumbled to the floor and rolled on his back like a beetle.

The commander bulged his eyes at this repulsive sight, then decided to ignore it. "At ease, Trooper," he ordered. As always, he was wearing his full-dress uniform, complete with saber, shotgun, sashes, ribbons, bullwhip, and medals that were really contraceptive holders, all this topped with an ornate gold-braid-covered tricornered hat. Reluctantly, he turned from the struggling Trooper and sighed.

"It's lonely at the top," he implied. "Just look out that window, Trooper. What do you see?"

"Stars, sir," said Bill. "That's about all anyone can see from this miserable place."

"Stars, son? Well, I guess some short-sighted unimaginative son of a bowb like you would only see stars, but I see glory. Yes, glory—and conflict! Warfare that pits man against Chinger. Great battles just filled to overflowing with heroic acts and doomed, selfless sacrifices. Facing death on a daily basis, doing what a man has to do, tests a man's mettle, wouldn't you agree?"

"If you say so, sir," said Bill, who fervently thought no such thing.

"Makes men out of boys, women out of girls, heroes out of cowards, dogs out of cats. Nothing like death to make a person feel alive. Of course, some of us, besieged by circumstance, must stand back and serve. Without us supplying them, the frontline troops wouldn't stand a chance against the enemy. Take toilet paper. Have you ever considered the strategic ramifications of toilet paper, Trooper?"

"Can't say as I have, sir," said Bill, who was beginning to wonder, and not for the first time, if the commander was playing with a full deck.

"Too much toilet paper and they'll have to jettison ammunition or fuel to make room to store it. Too little and they'll spend all their time looking for substitutes when they should be fighting. We could lose the war because of toilet paper. Sink the entire operation because they had to make room—*make room!* Just think about that, son."

Bill did, and decided on the spot that the commander's elevator didn't go all the way to the top floor.

"Making command decisions about toilet paper is a terrible burden. With one forged requisition slip the Chingers could destroy our entire armed forces."

Bill nodded, firmly convinced now that the commander was one brick shy of a load.

"Consider the mighty decimal point. With one slip of a decimal point. . . . Say, what happened to your foot? Aren't you the bowb who's been trashing my installation?"

"Doctor Hackenslash needs a new door," said Bill hastily. "And he said for me to give you this."

Commander Cook took the note and shook his head as he read it, his lips moving reluctantly as he spelled out the harder words.

"I guess I ought to go on sick leave," Bill said quickly. "Some extended bunk time would be best, just until my foot grows back, which—unfortunately—will take a long time."

The commander frowned. "I can't use a partial soldier at this station. You might get all worried about your foot-bud and load too much toilet paper for our troops fighting bravely on the front line and cause us to lose the whole ball of wax to those despicable Chingers."

"Bunk time sounds fine to me," Bill smarmed hopefully. "It'll be a sacrifice not to be involved with the war effort, but I'll just screw myself to the sticking place, grit my teeth, and endure it."

"I'm not sure that I like this screwed sticking place, bowb. Sounds subversive. So suggest an alternative," said the commander. "Something that would be right up the alley for an ambitious cretin like you."

"I could sit and count the boxes as the men load them," said Bill, thinking fast. "I'm real good at counting."

"No, I think I'll make you an MP."

"Empee?" asked Bill.

"Military Police, dimschitz," said the commander. "The *Bounty* is shipping out tomorrow on a salvage operation with a crew of hardened criminals. They need an MP to go along. Being an official Galactic Hero, you're just the man we need to keep them under control."

"Begging your pardon, sir, but I don't see that my presence would be necessary. Using Bloater drive they'll get there instantly. There wouldn't be anything for me to do."

"Quite the contrary. The *Bounty* is not one of your more modern ships. The truth is, she's a clunker, a space-going *Marie Celeste*—not much more than a primitive repair shop with a phase-loop drive strapped on it. The ship's destination is the Beta Draconis region, where our glorious heroic fighting forces have recently waged a fierce battle. The area is full of floating junk and half-destroyed spacers that need to be patched up to get back into the fray."

"So why send criminals? Why send me?"

"That's the beauty of the plan. It takes care of so many problems at once. By sending all my prisoners along I empty the brig and get rid of a lot of dead weight around here. Phase-loop travel is slow, and by the time you reach Beta Draconis their jail terms will be up and they can go back to work. Plus, your foot will have regrown and you'll be ready for active duty."

The commander turned back to his window. "I envy you this assignment," he sussurated insincerely. "You might even see some action. Of course a repair ship doesn't carry much in the way of weapons, so if you do get out there and toe-up to the enemy, it'll be in a losing cause. Such a noble way to die! How I envy you."

Bill stifled the obvious suggestion to change places and gave up. "I can't wait," he disgruntled, knowing there was no way out.

"Report to the *Bounty* in the morning. Captain Blight will be expecting you."

Bill had a real bad feeling about the whole thing.

CHAPTER **2**

THE *BOUNTY* WAS NOTHING TO WRITE home about, and from what Bill had heard, Captain Blight was even less. Still, Bill was determined to make a good impression and gave the captain his very best salute, the one using both right hands. Under normal circumstances it was an extraordinary gesture that never failed to dazzle, but its effect was somewhat diminished by Bill having to drop his crutches to execute the complicated maneuver and consequently falling to the ground in a thrashing and undignified heap.

"They send me a crippled MP. Wonderful." Captain Blight sneered incontinently, scowling down at the struggling Bill. He was a large man, heavyset; husky, thickly rotund, and stout; overabundantly gross to a degree Bill would have thought physically impossible. The man apparently liked to eat. A lot. Often. With seconds of everything. He looked Bill over with growing disgust.

"One foot, two right arms. Highly irregular. And what pray tell are those objects protruding from your mouth?"

"Tusks, sir, your honor," gasped Bill struggling to his foot.

"Apparently implants," said a voice from the door. "Not standard issue for *homo sapiens*. Of course they could be genetically engineered, or perhaps an evolutionary backslide. One should never commit oneself to a diagnosis from strictly visual evidence."

"That's sufficient, Caine," said the captain, painfully rotating his ponderous bulk towards Bill. "Oh, the things I put up with," he whined self-pityingly as he took a sniff of cocaine-snuff. "I've got a crew of criminals, a single, possibly alcoholic, surely decaying ex-Trooper to keep them in line—not to mention a fishbelly android science officer who couldn't make an unqualified statement if his batteries depended on it. It sure is lonely here at the top, being the only sane person around. Not to mention boring."

Bill looked around. The android looked considerably more human than the captain, certainly saner. Which wouldn't take much.

"Reporting for duty, sir," shouted Bill. "If you'll direct me to the brig, I'll check on the prisoners."

"What brig?" snorted the captain. "And keep the bowby decibels down. Repair shops don't have brigs. Those criminal prisoners are going to crew this vessel. And you're going to keep them in line and out of trouble, or I'll *make* a special brig for my *so-called* MP. Do I make myself clear?"

"Perfectly clear," said Bill, gathering up his crutches.

"Show this Trooper to his quarters, Caine," said

the captain. "I'll expect him at my table for lunch after we lift off this execrable excuse for a supply station."

Bill restrained himself and delivered a normal government issue one-handed salute, then hobbled out the door in the wake of the android, into the ship's corridor.

"Science is really wonderful, sir," Bill ingratiated, never missing an opportunity to brownnose, struggling to keep up with Caine. "A blessing to mankind. It can come in handy, too. This is the first ship I've been on with a real science officer aboard, even if it is an android. No offense, sir. Some of my best friends might be androids. I'm not sure that I ever met one before. I don't even know how to identify an android, unless maybe they smell too bad and glow in the dark. Hard to tell, you know."

"Please refrain from addressing me as *sir*," intoned Caine, with chilling android indifference. "In spite of any working title Captain Blight chooses to assign me, I am a civilian down to my last transistor. It's citizen Caine to you, if you don't mind, you racially intolerant simpleminded bowb-brain."

"Mind? Of course not. I am curious about one thing, though, I mean if it's not too personal a question to ask. You wouldn't be a . . . I mean one of those . . ."

"No," Caine shook his head and sighed deeply. "I'm not one of those cyberpunks. Cy-Pees have given the rest of us androids a bad name. For one thing, they're violent, and I abhor violence, that is unless the circumstances leave no other recourse. They're always plugging themselves into 220 circuits and blowing their logic boards. Juice junkies—no wonder their eyes shine like mirrors and their chips scintillate into the UV range. You will observe my ears are not pierced, my hair is stabilized at a fashionable length and tie-dyed, and my fingernails are clean. The Gibson mark IV with the da Vinci overdrive was the last Cy-Pee model off the assembly line, but it may be forever before the rest of us decent androids get a fair shake. Turn left."

"But you're not like them," said Bill quickly, pivoting smartly around the corner on his crutches. "You're a scientist, an objective observer of all nature's mysteries. A juice junky wouldn't have the attention span necessary to maintain the keen discipline required of all scientific investigation."

"Thank you for what I earnestly believe is a compliment, though I have my doubts because of your reduced brain capacity," said Caine. "But you have, perhaps, slightly exaggerated my experience. I am simply a horticulturist. Turn right."

"A what?" asked Bill, stumbling along in Caine's wake. "A whore what?" His brainpan was running a mile a minute, flooded with the usual Trooper's memories of missed opportunities and alcoholic detumescence, all jumbled up with the occasional opportunity that would have been much better missed than experienced.

"A simple botanist. A grower of plants. Green growies. *Kabish paisan*? Turn left."

"Plants?" Bill swallowed his bitter disappointment. "Plants aren't so bad. They're a lot like people, only they move slower. I was in the plant business myself once, in a manner of speaking. Fertilizer was to be my specialty."

"Fascinating," Caine yawned in a dry monotone, languidly lifting one eyebrow.

"It was a simpler time," Bill naffled nostalgically,

ignorant of any androidal acerbity and all awash with misplaced nostalgia for his home planet Phigerinadon II; remembering the plowing and the planting as some sort of noble back-to-the-earth venture and conveniently forgetting the crunchingly backbreaking pain, the long boring hours staring at the rust-eaten back end of a robomule. He'd never finished the correspondence course for Technical Fertilizer Operator anyway, and that time in the sewers of Helior was an experience better driven from his brain.

"Here we are," said Caine.

"These are my quarters? Great!" The room they faced was huge. Normally a repair bay big enough to hold a small ship, all the equipment had been shoved against the walls, leaving a great expanse of open floor. Open, that is, except for hundreds of beds of green leafy vegetables.

"What's all this stuff in my quarters?" whined Bill. "It's going to be hard for me to move around in there. Gotta clean it out—"

"Shut up," Caine suggested. "This is the captain's greenhouse." He led Bill inside. "It's his hobby, and his obsession. *Don't touch that!*"

Bill took the leaf out of his mouth and stuck it back in the dirt. "Tastes awful," he said. "What is it?"

"*Abelmoschus humungous*," said Caine, frowning and patting a little more dirt around the chewed-on leaf. "You might know it by its street name of okra. Big boy okra is what the uncouth call it. This particular variety is rather pulpy when mature, but it thrives under conditions of sandy soil. However, it does not do well when chomped upon before it has reached full growth."

"What's this stuff here?" asked Bill, walking over

to the next raised bed, prodded on by transient memories of his agricultural youth.

"*Abelmoschus gigantis*: Butter crunch okra," said Caine. "Rather misnamed, if you ask my opinion. Not a crunch in the bunch. A soggy mess, no matter how it is prepared."

"And that over there?"

"*Abelmoschus abominamus*: Honey blossom okra. Tastes like turpentine. One of the captain's favorites."

"It would be. And that?"

"*Abelmoschus fantomas*: Banana ear okra. Known for its insect-killing properties, if not for its completely unforgettable taste."

"And all the rest of these?" Bill swung one of his right arms, the black one, in a sweep around the room.

"Okra, okra, and more okra. Four hundred and thirty-two raised beds of okra. For an amateur, the captain pursues his hobby with impressive vigor. Of course, he's got me to do the scut-work, so that helps as far as he's concerned." It whined a high-pitched androidal whine of self-pity. "You have no idea how much time it takes to fertilize four hundred and thirty-two raised beds, no you don't, and that's not to mention weeding, thinning, and maintaining a normal cycle of watering . . ."

Suddenly, about a thousand overhead actinic lights crackled on. The temperature instantly rose thirty degrees and sweat burst in torrents from every pore on Bill's body.

"What's going on?!" he gasped.

"High noon," said Caine with a humorless smile. "Right on time. The captain runs a tight ship and—this is important to you but not to me—it also means we've got liftoff in thirty seconds. Oh, how time does fly when I'm with my plants. Lay down on this bag of potting soil instantly or you'll get squashed flat and you'll be no good for anything but the compost heap."

Bill barely had time to do a belly flop on the bag of stinking potting soil before all the G-forces started piling on top of each other, threatening to turn him into compost-bait. As it was he gasped and gurgled and was okay until the bag broke and he sank into the noisome mass it contained.

"I can't stand it!" shrieked Bill. "The smell!"

"You'll get used to it," smiled Caine, still standing, his tungsten steel skeleton impervious to the acceleration. "The smell goes away after a few days. It's all those wonderful nutrients, you know. Plants just love them."

"I hate them!" yelled Bill, though truth to tell, at the moment he hated phase-loop drive even more. That outmoded method of space travel had gone out with spats and shaved heads. There was no need to get squashed into compost when a modern drive would get you anyplace in no time at all in relative comfort.

Just when he couldn't take it anymore, the crushing forces of acceleration ceased, leaving him weak and sick to his stomach. Being encased in a broken bag of stinking potting soil did nothing to improve the state of either his mind or his stomach.

"My quarters," Bill moaned, dragging himself to his foot and knocking lumps of poorly sifted, rotting dirt from his uniform. "I've got to shower and disintegrate my clothes. Not to mention I might take a minute off and throw up."

"No time," yodeled Caine gleefully, bent over a raised bed and thinning okra with a practiced, professional hand. "We have a lunch engagement with the captain."

"But—"

"The captain runs a tight ship," smirked Caine. "Everything goes by the book, and the book goes by the clock. Right now the clock says lunch."

After a hurried walk, Bill sat down at the captain's table and eyed his plate with mounting suspicion. The mound of boiled okra looked a lot like the mass of limp steamed okra that snuggled up next to it. He tried the fried okra and almost broke a tusk on it. Everything in front of him was either too soggy to eat with anything but a spoon or too hard to eat period. He sighed and reached for his wine glass, took another sip of fresh-pressed okra juice.

The captain, sniffing the air doubtfully, was eyeing Bill with much the same expression Bill reserved for his plate of so-called food. The other two people at this dubious feast were Caine and the First Mate, a Mr. Christianson who had arrived at the last minute in a personal cruiser bearing the Emperor's seal. Of the four, only the captain had anything but okra on his plate.

"I say, is the air always like this?" asked Mr. Christianson, drawing a scented handkerchief from his ruffled sleeve and waving it in front of his nose. "It smells remarkably like a garbage scow in here." He glared at Bill and took a big spoonful of boiled okra, eating it with relish.

"How come I didn't get any relish?" asked Bill. "Some condiments might make this stuff go down a little easier. Mind passing me that horseradish?"

"I run a tight ship," said Blight, cutting a big juicy chunk off his steak. "Just as there are levels of command and responsibility, there are levels of largess, dispensed, of course, by myself. This is absolutely necessary to maintain discipline aboard my ship. You will notice that Mr. Christianson, by virtue of being First Mate, has full access to the condiment tray as well as having wine with his meals. Caine would be eligible for wine, but not condiments, though his metabolism is such that he cannot partake of spirits. Something to do with the effects of alcohol on his circuit boards, I believe. More's the pity. The wine is quite excellent."

"What about me?" asked Bill, eyeballing the wine and sipping his sour okra juice.

"Being closest to the crew, you get basically the same rations they do," said Blight, tearing a roll in half and dipping it in his mashed potatoes and gravy. "In my experience, that will help you in dealing with them. Keep you lean and mean and on your toes, so to speak. However, since you are the only Trooper aboard who isn't serving out a sentence for criminal activity, I have decided you are eligible for a fringe benefit. It will help remind you of your favored position."

"Benefit—tell me!" Bill slobbered, dreaming of the occasional steak, or maybe even a greasy, succulent porkuswine ham.

"As long as you remain in my good graces, you will be eligible for dessert," Blight said with an expansive smile.

"Dessert?"

"Jelly doughnuts," said Caine. "I think you will find them a welcome palate cleanser after an okra repast. Although I don't require much in the way of food, I enjoy them myself, especially those little raspberry fellows."

"Only one," said Blight, shaking a fork at Bill.

"Mr. Christianson and Caine each get two. I get six, on account of it's lonely at the top. You've got to clean your plate before you get any dessert, Trooper. I'd get cracking if I was you, which—thankfully— I'm not."

Bill looked at the mess in front of him. The excess grease from the fried okra was congealing into a semi-solid pool of gray matter. He took another slurp of his okra juice and turned to the First Mate.

"Excuse me, Mr. Christianson, sir," he said craftily, changing the conversation and diverting attention from himself. "What was your last assignment?" The First Mate was a dandy-looking man, the chest of his braid-encrusted uniform covered with medals and ribbons. His powdered wig was a little off-center, but that only added to his rakish image. As did his strabismus. Cross-eyes ran in the royal families.

"Assignment?"

"Work, gig, job, station, base," Bill translated, in case the word was too complex for his teeny-tiny officerial mind. "Like what other ships have you served on?" He gnawed on a grease-encrusted sprig of fried okra. "It's possible that I might know some of the crew. Which would sort of make us like maybe ex-shipmates, possibly." He muttered into silence, saw that no one was looking at him, then slipped the indigestible tidbit under his napkin and lifted a spoonful of the slimy boiled stuff. "I get around," he added proudly.

"This is my first ship," said Mr. Christianson, happily raiding the condiments tray, heaping Karbuklian salsa and grated porkuswine's-milk cheese on his okra. "My uncle simply *demanded* that I take one voyage before I get my captain's commission. Myself, I think it's an old-fashioned idea, but I guess if Uncle

Julius feels that strongly about it, I ought to at least try."

"Uncle Julius?" Bill slid a glob of steamed okra down his boot while no one was watching.

"He's the Emperor's four-hundred-and-second cousin twice removed," bragged Christianson, hogging the wine. "He managed to get me this far without having to go through that boring basic training or taking all those complicated tests for officer's candidate school—rank *doth* have its perks—but he *insisted* I go out on a space ship before I captained one. Silly man, after all the money my family freely donated under pain of death to the Emperor's war effort against the Chingers, but if I must, I must. By the way, has anyone ever mentioned that you have a most offensive body odor?"

Bill brushed off a few more lumps of potting soil and looked out the viewport at the supply station slowly receding into the distance. Too slowly. It was going to be a long voyage.

It was an even longer lunch. He managed to clear his plate by stuffing all manner of ill-prepared okra in various pockets and hiding places—even slipping a few hunks onto Caine's plate when he was distracted. He eventually disposed of all of it and leaped on his strawberry jelly doughnut like it was the very last supper of all time.

Afterwards, licking jelly from his lips, he followed Caine's directions to his quarters. Captain Blight had offhandedly mentioned that Bill was in dire need of a shower, and if he hadn't had one by the next time their paths crossed, he'd personally stuff him out an airlock and make him breathe vacuum until he learned a lesson or two about personal hygiene. Or something like that.

Bill opened the door of what he thought was his room and gaped at the behemoth who stood, when he was standing, about six foot five, three hundred pounds, sitting on one of the two beds, bending a forged steel lamp like it was made of rubber.

"Excuse me, wrong room," said Bill quickly, backpedaling like crazy.

"You da MP, right?" growled the bear of a man.

"I guess so," Bill said, smiling insincerely as he hopped backwards.

"Then dis da right room," the monster macerated, biting off the end of the lamp and spitting the pieces onto the floor. "We is bunkmates."

"I'm Bill," said Bill, hesitantly hopping into the room. "Pleased to meet you."

"My name Bruiser Bonecrusher," grunted the big ape. "Nice tusks. And—hey!—you got two right arms."

"Good eye, guy," said Bill.

"One of them right arms is black," snapped Bruiser.

"We all can't be perfect," Bill ingratiated, crawfishing on crutches and foot toward the unoccupied side of the room. "If you're crew, what are you doing time for?" A change of subject might help. It didn't.

"Axe murder," hinted Bruiser, his broad grin revealing surgically implanted canines, two inches long and filed to sharp points.

"Could happen to anybody," said Bill.

"Cut feet off MP an' left him in snow to bleed to death."

"I know how it goes," said Bill. "Sometimes stuff like that just happens."

"Course, he had two feet. You just got one. Only take half time."

"You got to realize there's no snow on this ship," gasped Bill. "And none forecasted in the foreseeable future."

"That black arm you got remind me of someone," growled Bonecrusher. "Goes way back."

"Well, me and this arm go way back, too."

"Reminds me of big Trooper name of Tembo," grunted Bruiser. "He and I never get along."

"You and I will get along better, I'm sure," Bill implied hopefully. He remembered Tembo, blown apart in that awful battle, and how he awoke with Tembo's arm surgically attached to his body. A bit of news he was determined to keep to himself.

"He drive me bonkers, all that preaching. Voodoo day an' night. I mean to kill him, still got nightmares. But he shipped out while I was in da brig for like doin' something I forgot. I lookin' for him ever since. He ever lay hand on me, I chop it off in a second."

Bill watched his right hand, the black one, clench into a tight fist, and knew for sure it was going to be a long, long trip.

CHAPTER 3

BRUISER BONECRUSHER WAS THE MEAN-est-looking human Bill had met in his entire life, right up until the moment Rambette walked in the door about five horrible minutes later.

Rambette was of medium height, medium weight, and had medium brown hair. She stopped being medium right there. Her eyes were a blazing blue, and she carried all manner of knives and menacing weapons strapped in bandoleers wrapped around her attractive, curvaceous—though barely visible behind the armament—body.

"Where's that MP, Bruiser?" she rasped huskily. "We got a problem in Repair Dock Four."

"I'm the MP assigned to this ship, miss," said Bill, staring in awe at a gigantic curved scimitar stuck in her belt. "Bill's my name."

"I'm Rambette," she said, looking down below his belt and laughing. "You seem to be missing a piece or two."

In horrified shock Bill looked down—his zipper was closed! He relaxed and the cold sweat cooled on his brow. "Oh, my *foot* you mean. The doc said that it'll grow back."

"Nice tusks, though," mused Rambette, reaching over and twanging one suggestively. "Well, back to work. Bruiser, you better bring your axe. Larry's in one of his wild moods and strong measures might be called for."

"Dat's great!" grinned Bruiser, dragging an oversized door-busting axe out from underneath his bunk and swinging it in whistling arcs through the air. "Not used old Slasher in some long time."

Bill looked at the razor-sharp blade with dismay. He saw something that might have been a spot of rust, or, with a tiny bit of imagination, could possibly have been a few drops of dried blood.

"C'mon, Bill, we better get hopping," said Rambette with a saucy grin.

"Har, har!" grunted Bruiser. "Hopping! I get it. Har, har!"

Bill failed to see any humor in that comment, but he hopped along with the dynamic deadly duo, thinking that only in the military would the prisoners be armed to the teeth and the guard equipped only with a pair of bent, rubber-tipped crutches. Head of the list of things to do was getting a weapon or weapons soonest.

The repair docks were several levels down, and Bill struggled to keep up with Rambette and Bruiser. He was beginning to wish he had his stone foot back again. For all the trouble it had been, that hunk of petrified foot was a weapon of sorts. This Larry character must be one mean bowb if Rambette thought

Bruiser needed more than a scowl to get him under control.

"Who's Larry?" asked Bill.

"Just another criminal slob serving out his term on this scow like all the rest of us," said Rambette, turning right.

"What did he do?"

"He might not have done anything," said Rambette. "You see, he's a clone."

"No, I don't see," said Bill.

"There are three of them. Larry, Moe, and Curly. All clones. Three peas out of the same pod. Three nuts off the same tree. One of them busted into the base computer and gave everybody a weekend pass. They've got the same fingerprints and identical retinal patterns, so the brass couldn't figure out which one of them had done the dirty deed. They court martialed them all for it. It was kind of a family package plan."

"That doesn't sound fair to me."

"Been a Trooper long, Bill?"

"Too long."

"Then you ought to know fair ain't got one thing to do with it."

Bill could only sigh retrospectively in agreement.

Bruiser was mumbling incoherently and affectionately to his beloved axe, Slasher, when they entered Repair Dock Four. This was as large as the okra chamber, but filled with massive equipment instead of potting soil, which, to Bill's eyes, was a definite improvement.

"Hop this way," said Rambette, leading them down a metal staircase to the floor, where a group of people were standing around arguing. "Believe it or not, Larry's the one waving the crowbar in the air."

Bill found it easy to believe. His luck was going from bad to worse.

"It went that way," yelled Larry. "And I ain't tracking that beast down for nothing, no way. I got more sense than that."

Larry was a thin man with light brown hair and a sharp, angular face creased with so many wrinkles and worry lines that Bill knew he was a Lifer for sure. Moe looked just like Larry and Curly looked just like Moe who looked like Larry and so on.

"It's all your fault," said Moe, or maybe Curly. "You got careless. Let him get away."

"Who you calling careless?" cried Larry. Or Curly. "I swear, Dad should have dropped your test tube when you were just a bunch of undifferentiated cells. I just can't believe I'm related to you."

"Leave Dad out of this," said Curly, or maybe Moe. "That thing is out there somewhere. We got to do something."

"Everybody split up," said Rambette. "Find the creature."

"Ugh! Not me," said a heavyset muscular black man, shaking his head. "Count me out."

"*Everybody!*" said Rambette, brandishing a particularly vicious-looking knife. "And that includes you, Uhuru. That's a direct order from Bill, our new MP, isn't it?"

"Uh, sure," said Bill, who was still trying to figure out Larry, Moe, and Curly. He'd lost track when Larry set the crowbar down. He thought Curly had it now, but it might have been Moe.

"A week of bread and water for any cowardly slackers. Right, Bill?"

"No less. We want no slackers here," said Bill, who was beginning to suspect that Larry himself had

picked the crowbar up again just to confuse him.
Confusing MPs had a long and honorable tradition
behind it.

"*Go!*" cried Rambette. "Look everywhere."

Bill was jolted into action, dropped one crutch, and
grabbed a wrench from a tool box. Everyone had
scattered and he was alone, armed with a wrench and
a crutch, staring down a long, deserted corridor. He
started out slowly, quietly.

The ceiling of the repair dock was far above him,
almost lost in a maze of suspended walkways, ele-
vated tracks, and all sorts of massive equipment.
Huge loops of chains hung down like giant spider
webs, clinking softly as they swayed back and forth.

Bill was wondering if the wrench would be enough
to handle the . . . the . . .

Agh! He didn't have any idea what kind of a monster he was chasing, or even how big it was. Fangs?
Claws? Bigger than a bread box? Smaller than a tank?
It could be hiding anywhere. Sweat burst from every
pore, which made it even worse. Now the thing could
track him by smell!

Maybe it was some horrible alien creature covered
with scales, lurking right around the next corner,
ready to pounce and tear him limb from limb. Maybe
it was a deadly praying mantis grown to impossible
size and at this very moment was staring coldly down
at him from above, all set to strike. Giant ants
and killer bees as big as a man were also possibilities
Bill considered, cursing his overactive imagination
and trembling with fear, eyes darting every which
way, nostrils flared. Very busy. He pressed on, fig-
uring the odds were better if he kept moving.

He turned a corner and looked up. A drop of water
hit his face, then another. The floor was wet and

slippery. The water tasted faintly of okra.

Bill was facing a long series of lockers, all closed tightly save one, which was slightly ajar. He approached it warily.

Where was everybody else? Bill had never felt so alone, so vulnerable. The repair dock was quiet as a tomb, save for the soft metallic clinking of the chains, the rhythmic dripping water, and the sound of labored breathing.

Labored breathing!? His heart began to pound like a trip-hammer, so loud he knew that the creature of evil out there could hear it!

He stopped, his crutch an inch away from swinging the locker door open, his wrench at the ready in his other right hand. He held his breath and the soft, muffled labored breathing stopped. He exhaled and it started again. An echo? Once more he held his breath. This time the breathing got louder, became a growl.

Suddenly the locker door burst open and something wet and slimy covered his face, blinding him. He was knocked backwards by a huge, crushing weight. A horrible rotting smell engulfed him.

"Help!" he yelled, smothering in slime. "I'm a goner!"

"Bill found the dog!" cried Larry, Moe, or Curly. "Boy, does he stink!"

"Dog?" said Bill, wiping dog slobber from his eyes. "Dog?"

"We tried to get a ship's cat," said Rambette, "but all the cats were checked out and this is what they stuck us with. Barfer is an awful dog."

Bill sat up and stared into the baleful eyes of an oversized sheepdog kind of a mongrel. His multi-colored, hyenalike fur was coming out in mangy handfuls. The creature had a stupid, grinning expression and his huge tongue was lolling out of the side of his mouth, dripping copious amounts of dog slobber. He gave Bill another big lick across his forehead, wagging his tail happily.

"Barfer likes you," said the large black man, giving Bill a hand and helping him to his feet. "That makes you a majority of one, on account of none of us can stand to be around him. My name's Uhuru, and I'm pleased to meet you. Looks like you got yourself a dog."

"I what?" said Bill.

"He stays your side of da room," Bruiser snarled, leaning on Slasher. "I find him on my bunk, chop his smelly legs off. Then start on yours."

"He does kind of stink," Bill admitted. "Thanks for the offer—but I don't need a dog."

"He needs you, and that is a law of nature that cannot be changed," a short and zoftig woman intoned ominously. "It is also Barfer's nature to roll around in the compost bin in the captain's okra room. We can't keep him out of there. Maybe you'll have better luck."

"Thanks," said Bill. "What's your name?"

"Tootsie, big boy. And what's yours?" She ran delicate fingers through her short-cropped blond hair and took a deep breath that impressed Bill immensely. She didn't look like a dangerous criminal, not in the slightest.

"Bill. With two L's. The same as the officers spell it." Then he remembered the call of duty. "What are you in for?" he asked, putting on his serious MP face.

"They say I deserted. Went AWOL. Over the hill. Hit the road."

"Did you?"

"Of course not. My time card got demagnetized by a broken drink machine so it didn't register. I was at my desk the whole time."

Duty still called, like it or not. He forced his attention away from Tootsie.

"And you, Uhuru. What did you do to get stuck here?"

"They charged me with blowing up an orphanage," he said with a wide grin. "I'm a big fan of gunpowder."

"Gunpowder?" asked Bill, staring at the heavily muscled arms of the huge man. "Orphanage? Little kids and all that?"

"I was framed," said Uhuru. "All I really did was accidentally drop a homemade firecracker down the officer's latrine. It made a big bang, but there weren't no orphans in sight, just a lot of exploded waste products and a very nervous lieutenant."

"Rambette?"

"They say I have a violent personality, believe it or not. And all on account of a little misunderstanding."

"Misunderstanding?"

"A corporal took me out to dinner. How romantic, I thought, I was so young and innocent. He embraced me, rained kisses on my fresh lips, ran his fingers down my . . . that kind of thing. Filled with fear and trepidation I threatened to cut one of them off for him and he got a little upset. But would not desist. In self-defense I rejected his advances. He was out of his cast inside two months. I didn't do anything but protect myself. It was nothing to get all excited about."

"That sounds reasonable," Bill adjudicated. "Larry?"

"Ask Moe."

"Moe?"

"Ask Curly."

"Curly?"

"I don't know nothing. And if I did know something, I'd blame it on Larry. Or maybe Moe. As far as I know, we are all innocent, just victims of a passing bad time. Of course, I can only speak for myself. I can't remember the last time we three agreed on anything. Larry's dumb as a rock, and Moe's a blight on the family tree."

"All these sound like minor infractions," said Bill. "Or maybe no infractions at all. I don't think we'll have any trouble this trip. All we've got to do is keep our noses clean until we get to Beta Draconis. That sounds pretty simple."

Barfer the dog leaned heavily against Bill's good leg and farted. Bill, unthinkingly, scratched the creature's smelly head—then drew his hand away and wiped his fingers on his pants leg.

"Me," said Bruiser. "You forget me."

"Just coming to you, good buddy," Bill smarmed. "What did you *really* do?"

"Cut legs off MP," grinned Bruiser. "Me and Slasher did right fine job."

Bill swallowed hard and smiled ingratiatingly.

"But I had good reason," leered Bruiser, hefting Slasher up to his shoulder.

"I'm sure you did," said Bill with relief.

"Bowb made me mad," smiled Bruiser. "And he had smelly, ugly dog."

CHAPTER 4

BILL STIRRED THE LAST OF HIS STEAMED okra around on his plate. It was cold, and had the consistency of month-old celery that had been cooked in a nuclear reactor and then left in the desert sun to decompose.

Five weeks of okra so far, and no end in sight! Bill shuddered. He would even have welcomed some loathsome Trooper chow as a change of pace. The only consolation was that his foot bud was finally beginning to grow out. That was the good news; the bad news was that it was growing out a little strange. For starters, so far it was gray in color, rather than a healthy pink. And there wasn't the hint of a toe yet; just a gray lump a little smaller than his fist. But at least it was long enough so that he could stumble on it, and he had packed away his crutches, hopefully forever. He'd give it time. One thing the military had was plenty of time.

"So how is the crew, Trooper?" asked Captain

Blight, greedily downing a porkuswine chop.

"All in order, sir," lied Bill.

He'd learned another lesson: don't rock the boat. Only last week he had tremblingly brought the captain the crew's demands that a change of diet could possibly be in order. The end result of that fiasco had been the withholding of Bill's jelly doughnut for three meals and an imposed day of fasting for the crew. The whole episode had done nothing to improve anyone's morale.

The truth was the crew was getting angry, hot-tempered, short-fused, balky, and sullen. That was on even-numbered days. On odd-numbered days they were obstinate and grouchy and testy. At the best of times they were simply cranky. Bill was caught in the middle and blamed it on bad vibrations, the okra—and their criminal records.

Bill slid the last spoonful of slime into his pocket. Just about the only good thing about his new dog was that Barfer liked okra, loved it, drooled and slobbered over it in a disgusting manner. He was, besides Christianson and Caine, the only creature aboard who could stand the stuff. Of course, Christianson would eat anything, and the reliability of Caine's android taste buds, if he even had any, were open to question.

A dog was the last thing Bill wanted or needed, but he was stuck with Barfer, at least for the duration of the trip. No one else would have anything to do with him. The only saving grace was that the beast had just enough residual sense of survival to stay on Bill's side of the room. Bruiser tended to sit, fondling his axe and glaring at the sordid hound. A steady vegetable diet had done nothing to improve Bruiser's state of mind.

"Aphids," said Caine as the jelly doughnuts were

being distributed. "And little green caterpillars, too. Sorry, Captain."

"Say *what!*" yelled Blight. "Not again!"

"It's a natural progression in a closed environment such as we have aboard ship," said Caine. "They have no predators to kill them off."

"I've got a whole ship full of predators," said Blight, taking a second doughnut. "Bill, get another bug-picking crew together."

"Pepper," suggested Bill. "Back on the farm we used to use a mixture of soap and pepper to control pests. It's easier than picking them off one by one. That's the way we did it when I was young . . ."

"Enough of your sickening bucolic memoirs," sneered Blight. "Easier! Who said anything about wanting it easier? Prisoners aren't supposed to have it easy. There is crime, therefore punishment."

"It's ecologically sound and mostly organic," said Bill hopefully. There was a very real possibility the crew might string him up if he had them picking bugs again.

"I do not wish to have pepper sprayed on my plants," said the captain. "It would destroy their tender and delicate flavor."

Bill refrained from mentioning the obvious: that Blight never ate okra and wouldn't have the faintest idea what it tasted like. The addition of copious amounts of pepper could only improve its palatability. Even the soap would help.

Bill was proved right. The crew frothed with anger when he told them they were pulling bug-picking duty. The only thing that saved him this time was the captain's threat of solitary confinement for malingerers, lasting for the rest of the trip with nothing but watered-down okra juice for sustenance, plus a doubling of any protester's prison sentence.

"Can't they at least turn down the lights while we're working in here?" asked Uhuru, who was stripped to the waist and sweating heavily.

"I talked to Caine about that," said Bill. "He's willing, but the captain said changing the light cycle would ruin his experiment."

"My back hurts," moaned Tootsie, leaning over an okra bed to get to the aphids in the middle. "And if you want to know—I'm rooting for the bugs. They can have all this green gunk they want."

"Be thankful we don't have an infestation of thrips," Bill suggested. "Or white flies. They're so small we'd be picking them off with tweezers."

"Aphids aren't exactly giant-sized," said Larry or Moe or Curly. "They're hard to get a good grip on without bending the leaves."

"Don't hurt the plants!" yelled Bill, remembering how a broken stem had brought fifty laps around B Deck with full packs.

"Quit complaining," said a grinning Bruiser. "I *like* squashing bugs. It almost as much fun as bashing heads. I just wish caterpillars bigger; it hard to pull legs off these little bowbers."

"We're supposed to be squashing, not torturing," said Rambette.

"Each to his own," Bruiser suggested sadistically, holding out a caterpillar and watching it squirm. "Wonder what they taste like."

"Yuck!" said Tootsie. "Eating bugs?"

"It's all protein," said Curly. Or maybe it was Larry. "They probably taste better than the okra." On the other hand, it could have been Moe.

Bruiser started making a pile of smashed, legless bugs, chuckling gleefully to himself. Bill shuddered.

"This is no way to win a war," said Rambette, dropping aphids into a jar. "I'd like to know what a bug hunt has to do with ridding the universe of those rotten Chinger lizards."

"I'm with you," said Uhuru, collecting caterpillars. "Sometimes I wish I hadn't set off that little explosion. Me, a trained Trooper, reduced to picking insects off plants! We should be fighting, not playing in a garden."

"I don't know," said Bill. "Maybe those Chingers aren't all that bad."

"Are you kidding?" Tootsie said. "They're monsters. Chingers are blood-thirsty killing machines. They eat babies for breakfast. Raw. You going soft on us?"

"I just thought maybe we ought to try to understand them," said Bill. "You know, open a meaningful dialogue or something."

"Only thing I open their stinking lizard bellies," snarled Bruiser. "Only good Chinger is dead Chinger."

"Have you ever met one face-to-face?" Bill suggested hesitantly. "It's possible they're not as mean as we think."

"I don't have to talk to them to know they're nothing but bad news," said Uhuru. "Killing them from long distance is good enough for me. Hit 'em before they hit you, I always say."

"I learned all I want to know about them in the training films," said Tootsie. "Vermin like that ought to be exterminated."

Bill sighed. It was clear the propaganda machine had done its work brainwashing the crew. He could hardly blame them, though, having thought the same way before he actually met one. Maybe he still did.

They labored on under the burning lights until one after another they moaned and dropped exhausted. "Time for a break," Bill said. "Take ten."

He needed a break himself. A stack of fertilizer sacks in the far corner made a shaded area that looked remarkably cozy. Bill stumbled over and sighed as he slumped into the relative coolth. His eyes closed, sleep descended—and something hot and heavy clutched him.

"Glumph!" he mumbled as something wet and burning sealed his mouth. He struggled free and scrambled back, looking up to see an angry Rambette standing over him.

"You don't like to be kissed, hmm? Maybe you don't like girls."

"Sure I like girls. But it happened so quick—"

"No need to lie!" she whimpered, sitting beside him with a clash of knives. "You don't think I'm feminine, that's it. Just one more warrior girl good only for battle. Well, it wasn't always like that. I was not always as you see me. Oh, things would have been different if it hadn't been for the bats."

"Bats?" Bill stuttered, batting his own eyes in confusion.

"Yes. If you let me hold your hand I'll tell you—

THE BATRIDER'S TALE

Ram-Bette set the gold-and-purple platinum band at her neck and slipped on her golden bracelets. Oh, this was to be a wondrous day when she and the other girls in Virgins Dorm Zash in the village of Smoosh on the shores of the Great Orgonne Sea—incidentally on the planet Ishus—at last had their Coming Out

Party. After this day she would no longer be a simple simpering girl but a full-fledged and proud Ishian. Oh, what a wondrous wakening.

"Tarry not, silly ones," ordered Drekk, suspiciously coy for one of her age and mien. "The ceremony awaits in the Great Hall."

They all sallied forth, trying not to giggle, and succeeding until Ram-Bam tripped over the feeble legs of a male who was floundering to get out of their way. This was too funny, and giggling turned to laughter until Drekk sniffed with offended dignity and they grew silent.

Oh, the Great Hall was as they had never seen it before! Lambent flame flickered from gilt sconces on the wall, reflected from the diamond eyes of the great statue of Dingg-Bat that filled the end of the majestic Hall.

"Silence, O Daughters of Smoosh," Drekk called out in command, and they were silent as the Elder Mothers filed forward and stood before them. "Virgins of Dorm Zash, today your destinies will be fulfilled. Today you will Come Out of Virginhood into full proud Status. In our fair language, as you all well know, Ram means mother so thus all your names begin with Ram, followed of course by your dear mother's name, separated of course by a hyphen, and on this most Sacred and Important Day we will take your hyphens away. You will be dehyphenized! Your new names will signify your new status. Some of you will become Noble Mothers to reluctantly but boldly mate with the feeble males of our race. Others with green fingers and dirt under their nails will become Farmerettes to grow the vital crops that sustain us. Others . . ."

Ram-Bette, soon to become Rambette when she was dehyphcnized, wanted to listen to every silver word—but was distracted. There was a strange and high-pitched sound that drew her attention, caused her to turn and gaze up into the darkness of the Great Hall above. Drekk caught the movement and her eyes widened and she gasped with pleasure.

"Ram-Bette, soon to be Rambette, step forward nobly and face your sister virgins. You have been chosen! Stand here, Dear One—do not be afraid, for yours is the noblest role of all in Smoosh. Because your voice has not changed like the others and is still high and squeaky. Because you have sort of a pin head with small ears and eardrums. Because of that, you and *you alone* heard the bat that was admitted to this Great Hall as a test. Only *you* of all who dwell in Dorm Zash will become that savior of us all—a *Batrider*."

The Ceremony was tragic, turgid, illuminating, and fulfilling. Afterwards, when all the others had gone, Rambette stood before Drekk, under the brooding statue of Dingg-Bat, and Swore the Oath of Fealty, drank the Wine of Dingg, which made her head swim in giddy circles, then and only then, was she told the Secret of Secrets.

"I have sealed the Entrance Portal and put out the Do Not Disturb sign," Drekk intoned. "Now the Secret of Secrets can be revealed. This village of Smoosh has not been founded on the shores of the Great Orgonne Sea by chance. You must understand that Ishus is a watery planet and covered with a Great Ocean. Lo, many, many parsecs ago our ancestors settled this land, coming here from across the Sea of

Space, we know not how. All was peaceful, or so it was written, for many golden years. But then the Bad Years came.

"Strange chemicals leaking from the planet's core were activated by strange radiation from the sun. These caused gene changes, or so our Wise Ones say, for I myself know naught of such mysteries. The X chromosome of the males was stunted and crunched, which is why all men are stunted and crunched and die young and are worthless except for their single function of which I shall tell you anon. The Y chromosome of the female was made radiant by the radiation, which is why we are so big and radiant. But—alas!—there was a hideous mutation and the muscular and grim Z chromosome split from the other two. Those who possess the Z chromosome are muscular and grim and women—but with a difference. The Sacred Diagram of the Mendelian Triangle demonstrates this. When X and Z cross there is dominant and recessive and since women are dominant more women are born, and of course a few feeble men, which is all we need. But a Z chromosome is dominant and when these cross only women with Z chromosomes are born. Do you understand the significance of this?"

Rambette, who had been listening in stupefied awe, had not an inkling of what Drekk was talking about. She gurgled dashingly, shook her head, then nodded.

"I know it is difficult," Drekk intoned. "But in time you will learn all. Suffice to say now that only females with Z chromosomes are born of women with Z chromosomes. And in this fact lies the unhappy history of our fair world. It is written that there was a Battle of the Sexes between those of the Y and those of the Z. It was fierce and deadly and in the end the Outsiders, as those with the Z chromosome came to be called, were driven from this land, angry and manless, doomed to die away at last since none were born to replace them.

"But, oh, the muscular grim Outsiders also had an Unholy intelligence. Driven though they were into the Great Swamps they persevered. With great ingenuity they felled trees and bound them with vines until they constructed a Great Seagoing Raft. They built an earthen dike around the edge of this raft to prevent the waves from washing over and swamping it, and launched it into the sea, and thus escaped certain death at our hands. Nor does the story end there! The currents in the ocean are such that although this Dikeworld circles far from land, every twenty years it is pushed back ashore. Then hideous battle is joined as we fight to hold onto our feeble men, and these battling warriors fight to steal them from us. For endless years we lost these battles. Many of our men were stolen. The Outsiders prospered whilst our numbers waned. Then the first Giant Bats were found in caverns by the sea. Girls like you—with high-pitched voices and keen hearing—were trained to ride those bats in battle. Thus were the Batriders born!"

Rambette stopped the story when she felt Bill pull his hand from hers.

"Time to work," he said. "Break's over. You can tell me the rest of the story later."

"Story!" she frothed. "Here I am revealing my true nature, my secrets—and you say *story*!" Sharp knives were suddenly in her hands, instant death in her eyes.

"I didn't mean that!" Bill squealed. "I meant we

should be working, but what you have told me is so important that I want to hear more."

"That's better." The knives vanished. "I will tell you all, in greatest detail, when we are alone again. Tell you of the years of Battraining, learning to speak to those great hairy, tick-ridden creatures. Learning how to heal their wounds, comfort their young. How to hang upside down when mounting them. Then, oh how we fought, flapping and squeaking into battle. The red bats were vampire bats and were trained to swoop down and suck the blood of the Outsiders. The black bats were carnivorous and flapped furiously into battle, snatching dismembered arms out of the air when their Batgirl riders hacked them off with swords. But the most feared of all were the green bats, terrifying dive bombers. Those I rode proudly. Before the attack they would be fed on Tingleberries, great fruit filled with giant seeds. Then I would fly to the attack, holding a berry on a pole out ahead of my bat. Once over the enemy I would let the bat eat the berry. Bats' digestive systems are constructed so that when a bat eats fruit its sphincters open to make room. The old seeds are ejected and fall with killing force. My poo-bomber helped us win the war. But the enemy always managed to steal some of our men. Always more were born to carry on their race. Until the spaceship came."

"Spaceship?"

"Yes, an Imperial Scoutship. Bringing both good news to my race and bad news to me. They detected our settlement and what appeared to be an offshore island. They landed on it and Dikeworld sank and was no more. The scoutship lifted off and landed on the beach. I was the closest one when the port opened. And there was a man—I mean a Man! After the puny, crummy men on my world this broad-shouldered Trooper made me swoon with anticipation. He approached me and smiled. I simpered in return. He reached into his trousers and took something out.

" 'Do you know what this is?' he asked in a deep-timbered voice.

" 'I—I think I do,' I quavered.

" 'Do you want to hold it?'

" 'Oh yes!' I said stupidly. I took the fountain pen, thinking it was a present. Oh, how young and foolish I was! Under his guidance I wrote SWAK, sealed with a kiss in our language, and made a big X on the paper. Only when he had explained to the other Troopers who emerged from the craft that I had just enlisted did I realize how he had betrayed me. In a fit of temper I killed him on the spot, and the Troopers were more than happy to help me bury a Recruiting Sergeant. But—alas!—the piece of paper I had signed was found by an officer who found me—and that is why you find me here. And you do find me attractive, don't you Bill? . . ."

"Bill—where are you?" Christianson called out. "I see you. I want you, all of you, over here. At ease, troops." Christianson had arrived with the android, Caine. Everybody ignored him. The only thing Christianson had going for him was that he had the captain's ear. Which did them no good at all.

"I'm afraid I have bad news, Bill," droned Caine sadistically.

"All we have is bad news! We're getting fried by these lights while we break our backs picking bugs." Bill privately thought that the android had blown a valve somewhere, but didn't dare say it out loud. "It can't get any worse than this."

"Ahh, but I'm afraid it does," Caine enthused.

"Give it us straight," Bruiser growled throatily.

"They made a mistake back at the supply station."

"That whole supply station was a mistake," muttered Bill, wishing he had never set foot in the place.

"A serious mistake," said Caine, looking as sorrowful as it was possible for an android to look. "You know about the auxiliary water tanks, right?"

"The ones to water these beds?" asked Bill. He tried not to look superior as he acted superior. "Sure. There are ten auxiliary tanks aboard ship for the vegetables. They're Class AAA tanks, double-walled and triple-insulated, each holding two thousand five hundred gallons of water."

Bill was proud of the fact that he had read the ship's manual from cover to cover. Of course, it was the only thing to read besides gardening books on the entire ship, not counting the maso-sadistic porno comic magazines that Bruiser kept hidden under his bunk.

"You are correct that there are ten tanks," said Caine. "But there is more to it than that. An hour ago, having depleted Tank One, I switched to Tank Two. It was then that I discovered that the tank in question had been mistakenly filled at the supply station with olive oil rather than water."

"Olive oil?" said Bill.

"And not a very good grade, I'm afraid," said Caine. "At least a third or fourth pressing. In addition, it appears to be rancid."

"That sounds like the work of Commander Cook," said Tootsie, standing up and stretching her back. "If he's got a surplus, he ships it out any way he can."

"So we dump it or eat fried okra for a while," said Bill. "Big deal."

"Big deal is, unfortunately, correct," said Caine. "All the remaining tanks also contain olive oil of the same disgusting quality. There is no auxiliary water for the crops at all."

"Whoop!" cried Larry or Moe or Curly. "The crop is going to wither and die and rot! We're going to get to eat something different."

"The captain does not see it that way," said Christianson. "He will use the main water tank to irrigate his experiment."

"Is this some kind of a joke, Caine?" shrieked Bill. "That water's for the crew's use."

"It *was* for the crew's use," said Christianson, stepping between Bill and Caine, waving his scented handkerchief in Bill's face. "Let it be known that as of this moment, the crew is on restricted water rations. All water lines in the ship except those to the crops and the senior officers' quarters have been disconnected. An empty cup has been hung on the end of the robot arm in the ceiling of Repair Dock Five. Any member of the crew desiring water must climb to the end of the arm and retrieve the cup, take it to the officers' mess to have it filled, and return it to the end of the robot arm before it is refilled. There will be no exceptions. You may rest assured it is a very small cup."

"That's the stupidest thing I ever heard of," said Bill.

"Maybe. But it is also an order," said Christianson with a sneer. "Direct from Captain Blight."

"I'm sorry, Bill," said Caine. "I tried."

"You're too soft, Caine," said Christianson, turning to leave. "Let's go. And Bill—make that repellent chap put his shirt back on. Morale must be kept high at all times."

They walked out and the crew stood around, stunned by the recent turn of events.

"Do I really have to put on my shirt?" asked Uhuru. Bill shook his head gloomily. "Who knows—and who cares. I'm thirsty already."

"What are we going to do about the water?" asked Tootsie. "We can't make it without water."

"Mutiny!" cried Rambette, pulling out a dagger. "I say we mutiny!"

"That's sort of kind of extreme," said Bill. "Let me see what I can do first."

"Hey! These great!" cried Bruiser, tossing back a handful of bugs. "Give 'em try."

Bill watched his crew scramble to the okra beds, popping bugs into their mouths like they had never eaten before. Things were definitely bad, but mutiny? On the *Bounty?*

CHAPTER **5**

BILL HAD BEEN DREAMING OF WATER FOR
weeks. While he was asleep he swam ecstatically in
cool lakes, stood gratefully under the caress of gentle
rains and slurped satisfactorily at all manner of re-
freshing drinks. While he was awake it was quite
different. He was dry, parched, and chronically and
continually thirsty. Captain Blight had left them a
very small cup, and the robot arm seemed to get
longer and higher in the air with each arid, waterless
day.

He was worried about his foot, too. It wasn't doing
right at all. As a matter of fact, it was doing very
wrong. It had stopped growing, stabilizing itself in
a massive gray stump with large, flat toenails. It
looked and felt exactly like an elephant's foot and was
just as heavy.

Bill remembered Dr. Hackenslash's pachyderm fascination and shuddered. Surely he wouldn't have
gone that far. Caine, being a scientist android of sorts

and the closest thing to a doctor on board, with his knowledge of biology, had been no help at all, since Bill's foot was not made of plant material and therefore of little interest.

But as Bill opened the door to Captain Blight's office, his foot was the least of his concerns. He was worried. Why had the captain taken the unusual step of summoning him to his quarters? Attention from officers is always bad news for the troops. Blight usually had Christianson deliver his orders. It couldn't be aphids again; the crew was so hungry that the bugs never had a chance.

"At ease, Trooper," said the captain from his chair, almost invisible behind his rolls of fat. Sure enough, Christianson was standing at his side, sipping a glass of ice water.

"We have a serious problem," said Blight, looking grim. "A catastrophe of grave proportions has befallen us."

Bill's mind raced. No more water? An outbreak of mosaic rust virus in the okra beds? An endemic plague of Space Clap? Out of fuel? Lost in space? Marooned?

"A critical turn of events," said Christianson somberly. "Most severe."

"Are we going to die?" moaned Bill. Maybe they were being sucked down a black hole.

"Doughnuts," said Blight, the muscles in his jaw tightening, his hands gripping the arms of his chair, his fat all a-jiggle with barely controlled rage. "My doughnuts!"

"Doughnuts?" gurgled Bill.

"Gone," said Christianson, evilly clinking the ice in his glass. "Every last one."

"That's your catastrophe!" cried Bill, relieved they didn't have a black hole in their immediate future.

"I assure you this is most serious," Blight muttered darkly. "Somebody broke the computer code to the lock on the vault where the doughnuts were stored."

Bill gulped. That must have been Larry. Or Moe. Or Curly.

"Then the criminal wiped the protective magnetic strip clean," said Christianson. "Whoever did it knew what they were doing."

Tootsie. It must have been Tootsie.

"Then the thief sliced the main alarm cable," said Blight. "It's a very thick cable encased in steel. It would take an axe and a lot of muscle to get through it."

Bruiser! Oh no, not *Bruiser!*

"Next the vile perpetrator of this criminal act blew open the vault door," cried Blight, shaking his fist in the air. "A crude, but effective bomb. Probably homemade."

Uhuru!

"All the sealed bags of doughnuts had been sliced open," said Christianson. "Whoever did it must have used a razor blade or a very sharp knife."

Rambette!

"Gone," shouted Blight. "All gone, down to the last speck of powdered sugar! The vault looks like it's been licked clean."

Barfer! Was the dog in on it too?

"What do you think, Trooper?" asked Blight. "Do any suspects come to mind?"

"No," Bill lied instantly. "But if you want my opinion it sounds to me like a multitalented rabid psycho nutcase is on the loose."

"That kind of opinion I can live happily without. A psycho, maybe—but psycho or not, I want the culprit delivered to me in two hours," snarled Blight.

"I will not tolerate the theft of my personal property on this ship! Am I making myself clear, Military Policeman?"

"Yes, sir."

"I'm going to toss the perpetrator of this heinous crime out the airlock—*without benefit of trial or spacesuit!*" Blight roared, pounding his desk. "And if I don't see the guilty party standing right here in two hours, I'm going to start tossing people out into the vacuum until someone confesses. And I'm going to start with the MP. If you'd been doing your job, this would never have happened. Am I getting through to you? Get cracking."

Bill got cracking. He found the crew assembled in the room he shared with Bruiser and the dog. There were crumbs all over the floor.

"I can't imagine who could have done such a thing," said Rambette, wiping strawberry jelly off one of her knives with a rag.

"It was probably Mr. Christianson," said Uhuru, who smelled like cordite and had a fine dusting of powdered sugar on his shirt. "I never did trust him."

"Caine," said Bruiser, licking blueberry filling off his fingers. "He probably a factory second. Reject."

"Most likely Blight took them himself," said Larry or Moe or Curly. "That way he could have them all." The three clones had identical flakes of pastry glaze on their identical chins.

"Yeah, Blight," said Tootsie, brushing crumbs off her lap. "He's not one to share."

The dog Barfer crawled out from under Bill's bunk, looking guilty as only a smelly, flatulent dog with a big dab of raspberry filling on its nose can.

"It's got me stumped," Bill lied with heroic sincerity. Just then Caine walked in the room.

"I believe we have a problem," said the android, sitting on the edge of Bill's desk and politely ignoring the evidence of a recent pastry banquet.

"I'll say," said Bill. "I've got an hour and a half to come up with a volunteer for a space walk."

"The dog!" hooted Bruiser gleefully. "Blame it all on dat dumb dog."

"Barfer couldn't light a fuse," said Uhuru. "It'll never work."

"I'm afraid you don't have any more time," said Caine. "Captain Blight has become quite irrational. He has decided to jettison the entire crew and tell the authorities it was an accident. I think his metabolism is in disorder as a result of sugar withdrawal."

"I think he's plain bonkers," said Rambette. "He's a fruitcake. It's time for Plan Nine."

"Oh boy," said Bruiser, hefting Slasher to his shoulder. "I dig Plan Nine. Outer space!"

"Plan Nine?" said Bill. "What's Plan Nine?"

"Just like Plan Eight, but quicker," said Tootsie. "Mutiny!"

"Maybe we should just talk to him first," Bill equivocated. "I'm pretty sure he'll come around. Let's not be hasty. Mutiny is serious business and it looks bad on your military record."

"Stuff the military record! It's the only answer," said Larry or Moe or Curly.

"I've got it all down in my book," said Tootsie, waving a jelly-stained spiral notebook. "I wrote down every time he abused a crewmember. Remember that time Larry was too sick to climb the robot arm and Bruiser got him a cup of water and Blight caught him and locked him up for a week? I got that down. And that time he made Rambette scrub out the compost bin with a toothbrush? I got that down too. I got it *all* down. If we get out of this, no court in the universe would convict us."

"I don't know," said Bill, completely unconvinced. "Military courts always side with the highest-ranking officer and make sure the enlisted ranks never stand a chance. They're funny that way."

"How long has it been since you've had a cold glass of water?" asked Rambette.

"Well . . ." said Bill.

"And when was the last piece of meat you ate?" asked Tootsie. "I'll bet you can't even remember that far back."

"Well . . ." said Bill.

"Are you with us or against us?" asked Bruiser, standing up and towering over Bill, flipping Slasher from hand to hand like a pocket knife.

"Since you put it that totally logical way," said Bill, "I'm with you one hundred percent."

"I am also convinced," said Caine. "It's a somewhat logical answer to a totally illogical situation. And you, Bruiser," he added, looking at the axe, "do have a point."

"More like edge, har-har," grinned Bruiser.

"But that makes it unanimous!" cried Rambette. "Okay, Caine: *Mutiny!* Let's go!"

Captain Blight and Mr. Christianson were attempting to update the autopilot in order to find a good stretch of empty space to jettison the crew when Bill walked in alone, having drawn the short straw. Or rather, the short plastic tube.

"You're too late," snarled Blight. "Everybody goes, including you and that stupid foot of yours."

"Are you sure you won't change your mind?" asked Bill. "There's still time."

"There's no time," chortled Mr. Christianson.

"This ship is infested with thieving vermin, and we are about to exterminate all of you rats and roaches."

"I guess you leave me no choice," said Bill with grim determination. "I hereby inform you that a mutiny has taken place and you have been relieved of command."

"Mutiny?" laughed Blight. "Don't be silly."

Bruiser walked in and stood next to Bill, tapping Slasher's broad axe head against the floor.

"Mutiny?" gulped Mr. Christianson.

Rambette walked in, bristling with cutlery. "Mutiny," she said firmly. "Mutiny."

"Throw 'em out the airlock!" cried Tootsie, leading the rest of the crew into the now-crowded room. "Make 'em suck vacuum! Or into the hydroponic tanks—force them to walk the plankton."

"Wait!" said Bill.

"Yes, wait!" cried Blight desperately. "Please wait."

"How about a lifeboat, Bill?" asked Larry or Moe or Curly. "Let's set them adrift. It'll be a long, slow, humane death."

"There are no lifeboats on this scow," said Bill. "That's military economy at its very best."

"I don't see what you've got against killing them," said Rambette, "but if you're that set on it, let's just drop them off on some barren planet and get out of here."

"But how are we going to pilot the ship?" asked Bill, staring at the bewildering array of dials, gauges, and switches. "It's too complicated."

"Simple," said Larry, or maybe Moe.

"It's just another big computer," said Curly, or maybe Larry.

"One thing we know..." said Curly or Moe.

". . . like the back of our hands . . ." said Larry or Curly.

". . . is computers," finished Moe or Larry. Bill was getting confused.

"It's the only thing we agree on," they said in unison.

"Okay," said Bill with sudden determination. "Rambette, you and Bruiser lock them up in the okra room. Larry, Moe, and Curly, you all get busy on the autopilot."

"The okra room?" wailed Mr. Christianson.

"That way you won't starve," said Bill with a wicked grin.

"But will they ever be miserable!"

"But I'm allergic to okra," whined Blight, all aquiver with fear and loathing.

"Den you can eat da bugs," Bruiser sussurated, pushing them out of the room.

"How about that planet over there?" asked Tootsie, pointing out the viewscreen.

"The angry red planet?" asked Larry or Moe. "Good choice. It doesn't have any atmosphere. They'd go croakers in a second."

"No," said Bill firmly. "We turn them over to the authorities."

"No way," said Tootsie.

"Here's one," said Moe or Curly. "Not far, either, only a few days. It's ideal, an uninhabited barren planet with a communications station on it. We can leave them there."

"That sounds good," said Bill. "Head for it."

"A piece of cake," said Curly or Larry. "They've even got a message beacon transmitting for us to home in on."

"A message beacon?" asked Bill. "What is it saying?"

"I'm not sure," said Moe or Curly. "I can't quite make it out. It's either WELCOME or KEEP AWAY."

CHAPTER 6

"WHAT A DESOLATE PLACE, LARRY," SAID Bill, as they orbited the barren planet.

"It sure is, but I'm Curly," said Curly, happily punching numbers into the autopilot control board. "Larry's over there, programming the ship into landing mode."

"Then Moe—"

"You got it," said Curly. "He's the coward strapped into his chair with all that emergency webbing, the one wearing the crash helmet. He picked out our landing site."

The planet spun below them, a windswept derelict planet half a galaxy away from anything even rumored to be civilized. A continuous sandstorm boiled around the equator, the wild churning winds broken only by jagged mountain peaks jutting above the chaos. It painted a bleak picture: a dead world, lifeless and dismal.

"Is there anyone at all down there?" asked Bill.

"I can't tell," said Curly. "The only transmission we get is the message beacon, and it hasn't changed. They may have abandoned the station."

"Or they just might not be in a talkative mood," said Tootsie. "Can you really land a ship this big?"

"This is an old clunker of a workhorse," said Curly. "They don't make 'em like this anymore. It'll go anywhere."

"Yeah—but can you take it there?"

"And assuming that it holds together," groused Moe. "I don't like that storm."

"You don't like *anything*," said Larry. "Hey, Tootsie. How about passing me another baked porkuswine ham sandwich? On knakbread if it's no trouble. Lots of volcano sauce and maybe some of that tingleberry preserve. Programming is an energy-consuming operation."

Uhuru had spearheaded a frontal assault on the officers' mess, liberating a freezer full of exotic edibles and a pantry crammed with staples and luxuries. It had been carnivore heaven, meat with every meal and never an okra in sight. And full access to the condiment tray all the way to the nameless planet. Captain Blight and Christianson had settled down to a monotonous diet of okra and aphids, but not without wails of protest, said protest instantly overridden by Bruiser and his constant companion, Slasher.

"What do you think, Caine?" asked Bill, watching the storm below with all the fascination of a mouse staring down the throat of a hungry snake.

"It could be better," said Caine, shaking his head. "I would have preferred a planet with a somewhat more benign climate, not to mention botanical diversity. I'll be lucky if I even have some lichen to look at, which, as plants go, and they don't go far, are pretty boring. I don't mind saying that we may be making a big mistake by kidnaping and abandoning the captain and Mr. Christianson. Mutiny has traditionally been frowned upon with great enthusiasm by military authorities. On the other hand, a decision, once made, should be acted upon."

"In other words, you can't make up your mind," said Bill.

"Yes and no," said Caine.

"Going down in five minutes," said Curly. "It may get a little bumpy, so strap in and hang on."

A little bumpy? Curly proved himself to be a master of understatement, a veritable guru of erroneous prediction, and a pilot with a heavy and equally clumsy hand.

The *Bounty* hit the atmosphere with an earsplitting creak and an ominous groan. Every joint and rivet in the old bucket seemed to be under maximum stress. Bill hung on for dear life.

"More pitch!" yelled Larry. "Moe! We need more pitch!"

"No, it's yaw we need!" cried Moe. "Yaw!"

"I'm the one pushing the buttons!" roared Curly. "Don't confuse me! I'm having enough problems with the vector analysis."

"Don't confuse him!" echoed Bill from the bottom of his heart.

The ship was in a steep dive, twisting first one way and then another, whipping around like a leaf in a tornado.

"Roll!" shrieked Larry. "Give us some roll!"

"How can you think of food at a time like this?" called Tootsie. "I'm through fetching for you anyway. Get your own roll!"

"Forget the roll maneuver," bellowed Moe. "Give us a hit on the main engines!"

"We are encountering severe turbulence," called Caine. "I would advise a two-point-one-second burn on the starboard thrusters to stabilize the ship."

"Is starboard left or right?" wailed Curly.

"Left!" hollered Larry.

"Right!" cried Moe.

"What was that?" screamed Tootsie.

"I think we lost a shield!" Larry screamed. "The right one!"

"Left!" cried Moe. "Maybe starboard's left. Could be right, though. Which way's up?"

"We're going down!" quavered Bill. "Somebody turn on the exterior lights!"

Even with the lights on, nothing was visible through the viewscreen but whirling sand. Outside the ship the storm thundered and roared, sending borborismic echoes and vibrations through the hull.

"This is getting a little rough," called Rambette through the intercom from the okra room. "How about hitting the smooth switch?"

"Look!" called Tootsie. "There it is! I can see the landing pad."

"Piece of cake," said Curly, punching buttons like crazy and causing the *Bounty* to slip and slide sideways in a stomach-wrenching loop. "We got it made in the shade."

"We're gonna crash!" wailed Larry.

"Three hundred meters," called Moe. "Two hundred. Get ready! Hold on!"

"Who put the landing gear down?" barked Curly.

"That was your job!" moaned Larry.

"No, *you* were supposed to do it!" wailed Moe. "Do I have to do everything?"

"I got it," said Bill, pressing a button clearly marked ACTIVATE LANDING GEAR.

They hit with a crunch and a bang and a bell-ringer of a smashing jolt. Immediately, alarms started screaming and clanging. Flashing red lights filled the room with eye-destroying stroboscopic glare. Every WARNING and FAILURE light on the control boards glowed malevolently.

"I knew it!" yelled Tootsie. "We're done for! We traded slavery, tedium, endless heartburn, and monotony for certain death and total destruction."

"Bad trade," admitted Caine, unfastening his seat belt.

Suddenly the alarms all cut off at once. In the echoing silence that followed Bill climbed shakily to his feet and looked cow-eyed at Curly with newfound admiration and a sense of wonder.

"How did you fix all that stuff that went wrong?" he asked.

"I didn't," said Curly. "I just turned off the alarms. I hate all that noise."

"Look out there!" cried Tootsie, pointing at the viewscreen. "A giant snake is attacking the ship!"

A huge tubular object was winding its way to the *Bounty*, weaving and crawling on its belly like a reptile. When it got close to the vessel, it raised its front end up and struck the ship with a resounding clunk.

"We've been struck," chattered Bill.

"We've been docked!" called Larry.

"Tell me there's a cure for docked," moaned Tootsie. "I can't take much more of this."

"It is nothing to worry about," Caine pontificated. "That is simply an automatic docking tube connecting our ship with the communication station. We will now be able to pass back and forth without resorting to those cumbersome life-support systems with the funny little headlights and no relief tubes and the faceplates that always fog over."

"Damage report?" asked Bill.

"I think we got kind of a bunch of broken stuff," said Curly.

"Not too impressive," Bill sneered. "Can you be just a little more specific?"

"Sure. Some stuff is broken. Some things are bent. And this and that is not working like it ought to."

"Can we take off again?"

"Not without a lot of hard work," said Larry. "I knew it was a mistake to let Curly take us down. That clumsy bowb never mastered his first little red wagon, much less learned to walk and break wind at the same time. I can't imagine anyone less qualified to land this ship, except Moe of course, who's a total loss with anything more complicated than an off/on switch."

"Look who's talking," cried Moe. "You ought to—"

"Hey! What's going on?" Bruiser walked into the control room, leading Blight and Christianson by lengths of rope tied about their necks. "Can't a man catch a little sleep?" Rambette followed them all in, a knife in each hand.

"Sleep?" asked Tootsie.

"This concrete-skulled moron slept through it all," said Rambette. "Curled up nice as you please on an okra bed. Blight and Christianson were tied together and rode it out on the compost pile with Barfer. You may notice they have a certain aroma about them. Hey! What's that?"

"Docking tube," said Bill. "A walkway of sorts.

I guess we ought to check out the communication station."

"Who goes first?" asked Tootsie. "I volunteer for last!"

"There is a logical solution to this," Caine intoned. "If there are any military personnel out there it might be wisest for you mutineers to conceal that fact from them. True?" They all nodded like crazy except for the leashed officers, who snarled in revolt—and smelt revolting. "Since most of you are prisoners—and that fact could be in Galactic Records easily accessible by hand-held computer, none of the prisoners can go. As an android ship's officer you probably place little faith in me—that's it, nod your foolish heads off again. So that leaves our MP, duly appointed and theoretically next in line in the chain of command."

Bill stepped back away from the blazing pressure of all eyes turned on him. Bruiser spoke for all of them.

"Get out dere, bowb, and see what's goin' on."

The docking tube was a tight, twisting tunnel, and Bill reluctantly led the way, clumping along with his elephant foot. The others followed at a safe distance, reluctant to trust Bill alone. Except for Uhuru, who was staying behind with Curly to guard the prisoners and survey the damage to the ship, the two of them having been chosen by lot by drawing straws. Or rather, lengths of plastic tubing.

"I'm claustrophobic," said one of the clones, jammed between Tootsie and Larry or Moe. Bill had lost track of who was who in the clone department again—nor did he really care. The wind whipped unmercifully around the docking tube, howling and shrieking like a demented banshee. Bill had real bad feelings about this planet and not for the first time in his military existence wished that he was back on Phigerinadon II plowing the fields. But that time of youthful innocence was gone, lost forever. He'd been dealt a bad hand by the twists and turns of fate, but there was nothing to do but play the cards he had. Or some rationalization like that.

Still, he longed for a normal foot for a change, to ease his burden just a little bit.

"It's dark in here," complained Tootsie. "I can't see where I'm going."

"Bump into me and I'll lop off one of your limbs," warned Rambette.

"You were supposed to bring the flashlights," said Larry or Moe.

"That was *your* job," replied the other clone. "I was supposed to bring the lunch."

"Well, that means we've got two lunches and no flashlights. It's not my fault, either, knucklehead."

"Watch out who you call knucklehead, knucklehead. I've got half a mind to—"

"Wait!" cried Bill. "Hold it! There's something just ahead."

"I knew it," moaned Tootsie. "Monsters! The creeping unknown!"

"You got a death wish, Tootsie," said Rambette. "Give it to us straight, Bill. Can we kill it?"

"I doubt it," he said. "It looks like a door. Pretty substantial one, too."

"Perhaps you should open it," said Caine.

Bill felt for the latch and leaned against the metal surface. It opened slowly and reluctantly, hinges creaking. Bill carefully stuck his head inside and looked around.

"What do you see?" asked Tootsie.

"Nothing," said Bill. "It's pitch dark in there."

"How about I toss in a flare?" asked Bruiser. "I just love all that noise and fire."

"That's probably not called for yet," said Bill, stepping inside. "There must be a better way."

"Bowb!" growled Bruiser. "I don't ever get to have any fun."

"I would suggest we turn on the lights," said Caine. "Illumination would be to our advantage."

"And where would you suggest we *find* the lights?" Bill snapped sarcastically, getting a little tired of Caine's know-it-all attitude. "I can't see a thing."

"Light switches are usually located beside the door," said Caine. "It is the logical position for them."

Bill found the light switch immediately and when he clicked it on they saw that they were in what was apparently an anteroom to the main part of the station. A dozen spacesuits hung on a rack, and miscellaneous equipment was stacked against the walls. Several closed doors led off in different directions.

"Anybody home?" called Tootsie. Her voice echoed off the walls and died.

"This is spooky," said Larry or Moe. "Deserted. Why would they leave their suits?"

"I don't like this place one bit," said Moe or Larry. "Let's go back to the ship."

The dog came slinking out of the docking tube, his fur bristling. He walked over to Bill, smelling like compost and growling.

"Over here," called Caine. "Through this door. I've found the crew."

"Thank goodness," said Bill as relief flowed over him. "What do they say?"

"Not much," replied Caine. "They're all dead."

CHAPTER 7

"I'VE DECIPHERED THE MESSAGE BEA-con," radioed Curly from the ship. "I've sorted out the code. It definitely says KEEP AWAY."

"Thanks heaps," said Bill, following Caine into what must have once been a command center of sorts. "I suggest that you get down here soonest—and bring the prisoners with you. They might be able to figure out what is happening here." Passing the buck of responsibility in true military tradition.

A thin layer of dust covered everything in sight. Including the three men, shrunken and mummified, who sat in swivel chairs in front of a lifeless console.

"What do you think?" asked Bill.

"It appears that they are no longer functional biological units," observed Caine. "What we have here is three croaked people, unless, of course, we have something else."

"Like what, for instance?"

"Like something incredible from far beyond the

outer limits of human knowledge," said Caine. "We may be going where no man has gone before."

"Gross-out!" cried Tootsie. "What we have here is gross-out! I am going to faint..." She did, but everyone ignored her.

"These guys is all dried out," said Bruiser. "Look!"

He touched one of the mummified bodies with his axe handle. It immediately collapsed into a pile of dust and dry bones.

"Now you've gone and done it," Rambette said. "That's just what we need: a mummy's curse following us around."

"Technically speaking," Caine lectured, "a curse of that type can have no effect on a person unless they believe the curse will work. I myself am not a believer."

"I don't know *what* to believe," moaned Tootsie, who had recovered quickly when no one had noticed her. "This is a real creep show."

The prisoners, still leashed together, were led in. Captain Blight bulged his eyes with incredulity as he stared at the uniform and the pile of dust.

"What could possibly do a thing like that? That man was an officer. Enlisted men are the ones that are supposed to be exposed to danger, not officers. It's a rule."

"I would strongly suggest that someone—or something—is not playing by the rules," suggested Caine. "If I had to hazard a guess, I'd say it looks like their life force has been sucked out of them, along with most of their vital bodily fluids."

"Spare me the details," groaned Tootsie, looking sick.

"So what is dat we got here?" asked Bruiser, forehead furrowed in unaccustomed thought. "Sucked out like maybe big mosquitoes?"

"This is the work of an alien," said Bill with calm assurance, shaking his head. "Or, most likely, aliens, more than one. Or two. We're into something big here."

"Da bigger dey are—da harder dey fall," hissed Bruiser, swinging Slasher and accidentally pulverizing another mummy. "Bring 'em on."

"I suggest that we leave at once," said Bill. "We're in over our heads."

"I second the motion," said Tootsie.

"Third the motion," said Larry or Moe.

"Fourth," said the other clone. "Let's go."

"Uhuru," radioed Bill. "Come in, Uhuru. Speak to me."

There was no answer, only silence on the radio, dead silence, still as the tomb.

"Dey got Uhuru," shouted Bruiser. "Good old Uhuru, eaten by aliens!"

"I knew it," cried Tootsie. "This place is a death trap. We're all going to die!"

"That's a death wish, too," said Rambette. "We don't know for sure—"

"Uhuru here, Bill," crackled the radio. "I was in the freezer taking out some porkuswine chops to thaw. What do you want?"

"How soon can we take off?" asked Bill. "We got a small problem."

"No, you got a big problem," replied Uhuru. "There's a lot of busted stuff here. And what's not busted is all bent out of shape. We lost both shields and most every pipe in the ship has sprung leaks. Not to mention the toilets are backed up and the latch on the microwave oven is sprung."

"How long?" gulped Bill. "How long for repairs?"

"I figure I'll have the oven going in about two hours, three at max."

"Forget the oven, idiot! How long before we can lift off?"

"Maybe a week if we can salvage parts from the station," said Uhuru. "Maybe never if we can't."

"Think we got a week?" Bill asked Caine.

"Not a chance," he said.

"I'm hungry," Bruiser salivated. "Dere's nuttin' like trouble to make me hungry."

"We got extra lunches," said Larry and Moe. "Brought them special. Dig in."

"Real food!" cried Blight. "Meat!"

"Pass me one of those sandwiches," Christianson said slyly. Rambette glared at him.

"Please," said Christianson. "I forgot to say please. Sorry. Can I please have one of those wonderful sandwiches?"

"You can have all the okra you want when we get back. Now—watch us eat."

He did, moaning from time to time when someone belched happily or licked a crumb from their lips. The captain turned his back on the mutineers and scowled at the remaining corpse.

As they ate, Bill also looked over his shoulder at the one remaining mummy. There had been twelve spacesuits on the rack. What had happened to the other nine people?

"Give the dog a munch, Bill," said Rambette. "Barfer looks like he could use a bite."

"I tried. He won't eat it. He's on a straight okra diet by choice. He hasn't eaten anything else since that time he overdosed on doughnuts."

"I heard that!" shouted Blight.

"You heard nothing," snarled Bruiser.

"*I* didn't hear anything at all," volunteered Christianson. "I especially didn't hear anything about doughnuts. Can I have a sandwich? Please?"

"You can have Larry's crusts," said Moe. "Mister Macho over there always pulls them off."

"I've been thinking," said Caine.

"Good for you," said Bill. "What about?"

"Well, for starters, there's something strange about this place."

"I'm glad you noticed that," said Bill. "I would say a room with two dusted mummies and one more about to crumble would qualify as strange in anybody's book."

"Not only that," said Caine. "But why are we eating?"

"Because we're hungry," said Rambette.

"I, too, am hungry," said Caine. "That in itself is strange. As an android, I am not programmed for hunger unless my batteries need charging or I get low on oil."

"Maybe you need some volts?" said Bruiser.

"It is not necessary at this time," said Caine. "I believe something here is affecting our behavior. How else can one explain the fact that we are sitting here eating while our lives are in mortal danger and we're surrounded by mummies, intact or otherwise? It is simply not logical."

"What do you suggest?" asked Bill.

"First I think I'll have another sandwich," said Caine, taking one from the pile in the middle of the table.

"You may have something there," said Rambette, digging into the porkuswine cutlets. "Not only am I hungry, I have a sudden overwhelming desire to wander off alone and do incredible things even in the face of all this danger."

"Me too," said Bruiser, helping himself to more food. "But me, I always do stuff like dat."

"I never do stuff like that," said Tootsie, "but now I want to do stuff like that. You know: wander around in the dark with frightening things lurking behind every corner. For a professed coward, that's pretty odd behavior. I don't know what's caused our altered states."

"Maybe it's something in the dust," said Caine, wiping his finger along the table top and examining it. "It could be that this isn't dust at all, but mind-altering spores."

"Spores?" asked Larry or Moe, who had switched places around the table so many times Bill had lost track again. "What do you mean, spores?"

"I knew it," moaned Tootsie, brushing possible spores off her sandwich. "We're being attacked by killer mushrooms and we're all going to die!"

"That's death wish number three in the past twenty minutes, Tootsie," said Rambette between bites. "You really have a most negative attitude."

"I'll have to examine these possible spores in my laboratory," said Caine. "But first I think I'll have just a bite more and then take a little stroll all alone in a strange place."

"Curly, why don't you and Larry see if you can activate the console," said Bill. "Maybe there's a log-book in the memory banks that would explain what happened. Or maybe someone kept a written record."

"Good idea," agreed Rambette. "I suggest we all split up and search every dark, creepy corner of this place until we find something like that."

"Wait!" said Tootsie.

"Wait for what?" asked Caine. "Don't tell me you're afraid to go off by yourself and snoop around in dark and dangerous places."

"It's not that exactly," said Tootsie.

"Well, what is it?" asked Rambette.

"I'm still hungry," she said. "Would you please pass me some more?"

Bill got up from the table, stuffed. Barfer had wandered away, presumably in search of okra. Bill picked a door at random, opened it and stepped into a long, dark hallway. Having learned a valuable lesson in survival from Caine, the first thing he did was turn on the lights. They didn't help much. It was still dark and frightening.

Let's see, thought Bill. *If I was a diary or something like that—where would I be?* Probably in some loathsome corner, snuggled up to a killer mushroom.

Bill's new foot was starting to give him some trouble. Although it had stabilized in size, it was still getting heavier and had to be dragged most of the time. The skin was all wrinkled, ugly, and gray. It belonged on an elephant, not an Imperial Trooper aching for action. No standard-issue boot in the universe would fit the monstrous extremity. But at least its thick sole made footwear unnecessary.

There were slime tracks on the corridor floor and Bill wondered if that was a clue or simply a sign that Barfer had trotted down this very hallway, drooling and slobbering like he always did. He opened a side door at random and peered inside. Another mummy sat at a desk, all sucked dry. That brought the missing number down to eight.

Cautiously, he went inside the room, looking for

clues. It was a standard enlisted man's bunk: a cardboard dresser, a closet with a broken door, a contraceptive dispenser on the wall, a bed with a concrete mattress, and a mummy. On the desk was a thick black ledger with STATION'S LOG printed on the cover. In the closet were scratching sounds and the rasp of heavy breathing. The place was crawling with clues.

Heavy breathing?

"Barfer, come out of there," he called, walking to the closet. "Good dog."

No answer. More scratching.

"No stupid games and don't give me any trouble, Barfer," he said, grabbing the edge of the closet door. "I'll find you some okra."

The instant Bill opened the closet door, Barfer bounded into the room from the hallway, growling and barking. Something small and quick scuttled out of the closet past Bill. Barfer jumped into the air with a yipe. Bill jumped into the air with quick curses on his lips. And when he landed, Bill's elephant foot crashed through the floor.

"You scared me to death," he shouted at Barfer, who was standing on the bunk with his ears pushed back and all his fur standing on end, growling deep in his chest.

It took a minute for Bill to get his massive foot out of the hole. Then he peered down through the hole he had made into what he hoped was the basement. Wrong.

"Hey!" he yelled. "Over here! Everybody come!"

"Did you find the logbook?" called Caine as the sound of running footsteps filled the hallway.

"That's not all I found," shouted Bill. "There's

something under the station. It's huge! A cavern or some kind of a big empty place."

"Empty?" asked Rambette, busting into the room with a knife in each hand.

"Well, I guess it's not exactly empty," said Bill, looking down the dark hole. "Something incredibly loathsome and outstandingly repellent is moving around down there."

CHAPTER 8

"BOY, THAT LOOKS PRETTY KIND OF AW-ful down there," said Rambette as they all gathered around Bill's hole. "I can hardly wait to go down into the unknown darkness all by myself and see what's what. Who's got a rope?"

"I found a rope," said Tootsie. "And some atomic flashlights, too. But let's not be hasty. Maybe we should talk it over and get a plan of action."

"Smart t'inking," agreed Bruiser. "Dere could be plenty danger, alien bowbs, down there. Me first 'cause I da best. Me and Slasher, we take care of anything."

"As science officer, I am the obvious choice for the initial investigation of that repulsive place," said Caine. "No one else here has the necessary qualifi-cations."

"Slasher's all da quali'cations I need," snarled Bruiser.

"You're a *botanist*, Caine," said Larry or Moe. "I

don't expect we're going to find a bunch of killer tomatoes down there."

"Maybe we should draw straws," said Bill.

"That's stupid," said Tootsie. "Why don't we *all* go down there?"

"You're on," said Rambette, moving the mummy out of the way and tying the rope to the desk. "Here I go!"

"I just remembered—something ran out of the closet," said Bill, taking a flashlight from Tootsie and waiting his turn on the rope. "I really jumped. Barfer didn't like it either."

"Perhaps it was a space-rodent," said Caine. "A mutated ship's mouse or a giant fang-rat."

"No," said Bill. "It scuttled. Mice don't scuttle, not like that. Rats neither, I think. Whatever it was, it moved fast, too fast to see. But this much—it was positively scuttling."

"Hey! It's great down here," called Rambette. "And real threatening like in an alien sort of way."

"What about us?" Captain Blight whined. "You can't leave Christianson and me collared together like a couple of dogs."

"Sounds like a winner to me, hounds of a feather bound together," Tootsie demurred. Then changed her mind. "We'll take the collars off—but only if you come down into the hole with us."

"Done!" the two officers cried as one, chortling with joy as their restraints were removed.

"I no can wait!" bellowed Bruiser. "Me next. I got to go next. Maybe fight, kill—good stuff!"

"Anybody there?" radioed Uhuru. "This is the *Bounty* calling whoever's hanging around the radio."

"Bill here. How's it going?"

"Pretty good," said Uhuru. "I got the microwave

working and I'm cooking up a batch of popcorn right now."

"Oh—that's really great. You wouldn't maybe like want to tell us how's the rest of the ship?"

"I'm glad you asked. Pretty bad," said Uhuru. "Problems are coming to a head. I used all the duct tape on the ship trying to fix the toilet. If you find some more in the station, bring it back with you."

"We'll do that," said Bill. "But it may be a while. We're kind of busy right now."

"What's up?"

"Well, for starters, I was attacked."

"Attacked?" sneered Uhuru. "On a deserted, life-less planet? What was it, an invasion of the crab monsters? Mushroom people? Fifty-foot women?"

"Knock off the jokes—this is serious business. We're surrounded by dried mummies and there's a big cavern under the station, maybe full of whatever alien horrors killed the people here. We're going down to check it out. Caine thinks I was attacked by a mouse, but I know better."

"That's crazy," said Uhuru.

"No, I'm *sure* it wasn't a mouse."

"Now I *know* you're all around the bend," Uhuru whined intemperately. "You say you got dead people—mummies—scattered all around. Insane combat mice. Next you say you're going into unknown danger for no good reason at all, probably unarmed. That sounds like crazy to me. I wouldn't go down there with anything short of total body armor."

"We're not exactly unarmed," said Bill. "Bruiser's got his axe. Rambette said she'd share one or two of her knives with us."

"That's done it," said Uhuru. "I'm closing off the ship. Whatever mind disease you all have caught warps any good sense you might have ever had, which in some cases is very little. I don't want to catch it. I got enough trouble with good sense as it is."

"I feel fine," said Bill, getting ready to slide down the rope into the ominous cavern.

"That's exactly my point," said Uhuru. "You're going after some sort of a mummy-making monster with nothing but knives and you feel fine? Sounds fruitcake to me."

"You stand guard, Barfer," said Bill, patting the dog on the head, then wiping his hand on his trouser leg, and starting his slide to possible oblivion. The protesting voice on the radio got weaker and then gave out entirely as Bill disappeared through the hole in the floor, Uhuru rattling on about mind-bending diseases getting loose on the ship.

The cavern was immense, an impressive and intimidating grottolike cave of mammoth proportions. It was easily a hundred feet from floor to ceiling. The walls curved upward in a huge and graceful semicircle, lined with evenly spaced ridges. It was like being inside the chest cavity of some giant animal, or wandering around in a leviathan rack of ribs. There seemed to be no end to the cavern, and no beginning; it stretched out into the distance as far as it was possible to see.

Most of the above, however, Bill missed. He was so scared that he kept his eyes closed for the major part of the descent. Rambette helped him off the rope.

"This is a horrendous place," she said happily. "I've never been in a more terrifying situation. I guess I should be scared, but what I *really* feel like doing is wandering around and exploring on my own. See you later."

"What a great idea," said Caine, and wandered off as well.

"Hey, look at those stalagmites up there!" called Larry or Moe.

"They're stala*ctites*," said the other clone. "So named on account of they hold on *tight*."

"They're called stalag*mites* because they *might* fall on you. Everybody knows that, knucklehead."

"Who you calling knucklehead—"

"Hey—down here," called Bruiser. "Look at what I found."

Everybody who hadn't already wandered off on their own toward certain disaster came over to the giant riblike rock that Bruiser was standing on. He was staring down into a shallow pool that seemed to be filled with a translucent lime-green gelatin. There were things underneath the turgid colloid, lots of things.

"Ugh!" grimaced Tootsie. "Those are the most repulsive crawlies I've ever seen. What are they?"

"They look like decayed salamis stood on end," said a clone. "All leathery and wrinkled, slimily gruesome."

"Who would plant a field of decayed salamis, knucklehead?" said the other clone. "You can't grow salamis that way."

"Pods," said Bill. "They're pods of some sort. I wish Caine was here. Maybe they really are vegetables."

"T'ink dey good to eat?" asked Bruiser hopefully.

"They might be eggs," said Tootsie. "They look kind of like wasp eggs, only a lot bigger and more hideous in appearance."

"Eggs is good to eat," Bruiser grumbled. "But dose t'ings don't look so good."

"That's got to be some ugly chicken to lay eggs that look like that," said Tootsie.

"There must be thousands of them," observed Captain Blight.

"Millions," calculated Christianson. "Look over there . . . and there . . . and—everywhere!"

Sure enough, the entire floor of the cavern seemed to be covered with lime gelatin pools of pods between the riblike walkways.

"It must be a real busy chicken," said Tootsie.

"I don't think we're dealing with chickens here," Bill observed speculatively, leaning over the pool to get a closer look at the pods. "At least not *normal* chickens."

"Hey, this one has something moving inside it," said Christianson, bending over, his nose inches from a pod. "It's real disgusting."

"Dis one's moving too," said Bruiser, taking a good close look. "How about dat!"

"If you brush the gelatin aside you can see better," said Larry or Moe, on his knees leaning over the edge. "Of course you get gooey stuff on your hands."

"Glakk!" screamed Tootsie. "It's horrible!"

"Did you get too close to a pod?" asked Bill. "Did something jump out at you?"

"No, but I got some of the slime on me," said Tootsie. "It's awful."

"I think we ought to be careful," warned Bill, leaning a little further over. "There's something alien about all this."

"We don't know anything about these pods," said Christianson, poking one with his finger. "I think they might be dangerous."

"You could be right," said Bruiser, leaning down and sniffing a pod. "But I kinda like dem."

"I normally don't agree with criminals," agreed Captain Blight. "There's something forbidding and malevolent about these pods, but at the same time I'm fascinated by them. If I waded in the pool I could get a better look."

"That doesn't sound like a very good idea," said Bill. "Something dangerous would probably happen."

"Arg!" yelled Bruiser.

"Yipe!" burbled Christianson.

"What happened?" asked Bill.

"Something horrible—evil—jumped out of the pods they were looking at," moaned Tootsie. "The creatures wrapped themselves around their heads and won't let go. Come look."

Bill rushed over, being careful not to fall into a pool of pods.

"Kill it," he cried.

"I can't," she said. "I just can't."

"Is it some alien creature with an impervious shell?" asked Bill. "Is it indestructible?"

"No, it's too cute to kill."

Bill saw Tootsie was right. The alien creatures wrapped around Bruiser and Christianson looked like a cross between moldy teddy bears and little baby ducks.

"Are they okay?" asked Captain Blight. "Mr. Christianson comes from a very wealthy and powerful family. There could be serious repercussions if he were to be eaten by aliens while on a mission under my command."

"They're still breathing," said Bill. "And, P.S., you're not in command anymore."

"Oh, I forgot," muttered Blight. "It's hard to lay down the mantle of responsibility, you know."

"What happened?" said Caine, arriving with Rambette. "I was out wandering by myself, minding my own business, when I heard the bloodcurdling screams. Is something wrong?"

"You might say that," said Bill. "Alien creatures popped out of the pods and have attached themselves to Bruiser and Christianson."

"It was more of a jump," said Tootsie. "I wouldn't exactly call it a pop."

"Did it scuttle?" asked Bill. "I missed it."

"No, it sprung out," said Larry or Moe. "Just like a coiled spring!"

"It was definitely a leap," said the other clone. "Not a bit like a spring."

"Oh, they're cute," said Rambette. "Soft and cuddly. I wish I had one."

"You would regret it if you did," said Caine. "I believe that, in spite of their appearances, they're deadly."

"Deadly?" asked Larry or Moe. "Just look at those tiny little webbed feet and those cute little eyes, like little adorable black buttons. I can't believe they have a deadly bone in their cute little tiny bodies."

"These are alien creatures," said Caine. "Juveniles. As an android, I can recognize what you humans call 'cute' only in the abstract. I do, however, know that all creatures, great and small, have 'cute' babies. It is a protective mechanism for the preservation of the species. That way their parents don't eat them or leave them out on ice floes."

"I suppose they could be dangerous," said Bill

doubtfully. "As cute as they are, they seem to have messed up Bruiser and Christianson pretty well. The poor bowbs are just standing there breathing heavily and staring off into space."

"We had better get them back to the ship," said Caine. "I'll need to run some tests. I don't like the looks of this, but I think I know what's happened here."

The crew held their breath as one and bulged their eyes with anticipation as they all turned and looked at the android.

"The aliens are turning them into zombies."

CHAPTER 9

BILL DIDN'T EVEN BELIEVE IN ZOMBIES, and here he was, lugging one around. Of course, up until recently, he hadn't believed in mummies either. Life was sure full of surprises. Now he sweated and suffered and felt sorry for himself as experience suspended an entire lifetime of disbelief. Bruiser was heavy, and—being obviously part zombie—was not cooperating at all. Bill had the legs, and Caine and Captain Blight each had an arm. The alien creature more or less had the head to itself. No one wanted to go near that part.

"Got the sling ready?" called Bill.

"Coming down," said Rambette from the hole in the ceiling of the cavern. "Watch that it doesn't tilt. We almost dropped and splattered Christianson. Not that it would have been any real loss." She was all heart.

They strapped Bruiser into the sling and watched

as the crew pulled him up. Bill was looking forward to getting out of this place.

"This appears to be a nursery," Caine observed. "I wonder how many adults are lurking around here."

"Don't talk like that!" Bill suggested, swallowing his heart, which seemed to be lodged in his throat. "Don't even joke about it."

"It would be an edifying, and probably horrible, experience," said Caine. "Maybe even fatal."

"Shut your mouth except to put in food," Blight ordered caustically. "Fatal encounters with homophagous aliens are activities best reserved for enlisted men, not officers."

Bill watched Bruiser disappear up through the hole. The rope dropped back down and he caught it.

"You know Uhuru has sealed off the ship, don't you?" Bill said, finding something else to worry about as he wrapped the rope around his waist and held it tight with one of his right arms. "He's afraid of catching something."

"That's a logical action on his part," said Caine. "If I were him, I'd do the same thing."

"But since we're us," said Bill, "what do we do next?"

"Get into the ship," said Caine. "It is also the logical thing to do."

Barfer was overjoyed to see Bill again. As soon as Bill popped through the hole the dog knocked him down, covering him with obnoxious, slimy, slobbery dog kisses, standing on his chest at the same time and squeezing the breath out of him.

"We gotta get Caine up here fast," said Rambette, kicking the repellent hound aside as she unwrapped Bill and dropped the rope back down. "This is important."

"What's happened now?" asked Bill with gloom-filled expectation.

"We've been reading the station's log," said Tootsie. "Bad, bad news."

"I heard that," said Caine, crawling out of the hole. "What's the last entry?"

"Do we really have to pull Captain Blight up?" asked Larry or Curly. "I vote we leave him down there forever."

"I heard that!" shouted Blight from the cavern floor. "And I demand—"

"We might as well bring him up," said Bill. "At least that way we can keep an eye on him."

"The last entry is about a month ago," said Rambette. "It reads as follows: *This is horrible!*"

"And the one before that?" Bill asked trepidatiously.

"*This is disastrous!*" read Rambette, flipping pages. "And the one before that says: *This cannot go on much longer—the end! the end!*"

"I think we're on to something," suggested Caine. "I feel that something has gone wrong. Keep reading. Maybe there's a clue in the log."

"The previous day says: *It's appalling! Dire! Dreadful!*," read Rambette. "And the one before says: *Another dull day. Nothing ever happens here. I think I saw a mouse scuttle across the floor this afternoon.*"

"Scuttle?" cried Bill, suddenly alert. "Does it really say scuttle?"

"Read it and weep if you don't like the way I do it," sneered Rambette, passing him the log. Bill read slowly, lips moving, thick finger following and keeping his place. She was right. There was nothing ominous written in it until the scuttling mouse was mentioned.

"What are we going to do about these two guys?" asked Tootsie, pointing to Bruiser and Christianson, who were propped up against the closet door. "They're giving me the screaming meemies."

"We need to get them back into the ship," said Caine. "It's the only way we can save them."

"How can we do that?" asked Rambette. "Uhuru's got the door locked."

"We get him to open it," said Bill.

"How?" sneered Caine.

"Simple," said Bill. "First we split up—"

"Stop right there," moaned Tootsie. "I've had it with splitting up. Just for openers I have found out that wandering around by myself in disgustingly dangerous places has lost its charm since Bruiser and that pretentious creep got turned into zombies."

"We must find impermeable binding tape," Bill cried aloud. "Lots of it. There ought to be some around here someplace."

And there was. Larry and Curly found a whole locker crammed full of the adhesive rolls. They piled it in a huge stack by the door to the docking tube and called Uhuru, who proved to be singularly unhelpful.

"You all still alive?" he asked. "I figured you'd all be mummies by now."

"Would you believe zombies?" whispered Rambette. "Or maybe an exfoliating slime-creature from some black lagoon?"

"Shut up," Tootsie suggested. "He'll hear you."

"No, Uhuru. We're all fine," lied Bill ingratiatingly. "Are you ready to let us in?"

"Forget it, good buddy Bill," snarled Uhuru. "I still got what remains of my good sense and I plan to keep it. The door stays locked until Moe and I get the ship fixed and blast out of here or we die of old age, whichever comes first."

"How are the toilets?" asked Bill.

"No potty privileges—so don't try and get back in that way. In any case, yuck!" said Uhuru. "Don't ask."

"That bad?"

"Indescribable!" said Uhuru. "So I'm not going to try."

"You think that impermeable binding tape would help a teensy bit?" Bill suggested with casual insouciance.

"It would be salvation—but I'm all out," Uhuru despaired. "And the pipes are still leaking."

"We've got tape," said Bill. "Lots and lots of it."

"I don't believe you," Uhuru suggested—but his voice was shaking. "Impermeable binding tape, huh?"

"Hundreds of rolls," said Bill. "Enough to tape every pipe in the ship twice. That ought to cut down on the aroma considerably."

"In that case I *might* let you in," said Uhuru. "But you'd have to go through the standard decontamination procedure for at least five hours and sit in the quarantine room for several days. Of course, I could run the tape through the sterilizer and use it right away. You guys would have to wait, though."

"We don't have days to spare," whispered Caine. "We don't even have hours. We're talking minutes here."

"Sorry, Uhuru, that won't work," Bill said firmly, glancing at Bruiser and Christianson, who were leaning against the wall looking for all the world like mind-wiped zombies except for the cute little alien creatures wrapped around their heads.

"The decontamination procedure makes me break out in a rash," Bill lied. "Here's the deal—it's straight in with the tape or no tape at all."

"I don't know," moaned Uhuru. "Are you absolutely sure your good sense is back in working order? Not that you could tell. I don't want no brain diseases invading the ship."

"We're all fine," lied Bill. "In the pink."

"No," said Uhuru. "I can't do it. As much as I need the tape, it's too risky."

"Suit yourself," said Bill. "You're the one that has to breathe what passes for air in there."

"Suit!" said Uhuru. "That's it! Suit! I'll get into a spacesuit. That way if you've got what I think you've got, it won't get to me."

"Clear thinking," Bill lied strenuously. "We're headed down the docking tube now."

The flashlights Tootsie had found made the trip back through the tube considerably easier, but that was more than counterbalanced by having to drag along a couple of stiff possible zombies while packing several hundred rolls of sticky tape. Plus it didn't help that Bill's elephant foot was now getting to be a real drag.

Uhuru, wearing a bulky spacesuit with little headlights like an arcade game, plus a fogged visor, opened the door, and the crew immediately rushed into the *Bounty* before he could change his mind. He was grabbing up rolls of tape when he finally noticed something was seriously wrong with a couple of the returnees.

"Bruiser's got some sort of an alien wrapped around him!" he cried. "We're being invaded!"

"Actually, it's more the other way around," said

Bill. "The aliens seem to have the upper hand on this planet."

"And Christianson too!" moaned Uhuru. "How could you bring these alien crapheads aboard the ship? You promised me your good sense was back!"

"We lost our good sense for a long time when something strange happened to us. We think," explained Rambette.

"Obviously," snarled Uhuru. "And something even stranger would happen to you if I had a gun handy."

"Think of it as an unparalleled opportunity for scientific investigation," intoned Caine. "It isn't every day you have the chance to examine disgustingly attractive alien life forms."

"You're right, you're right," he said, tenderly poking one of the aliens with a finger and shuddering. "They are cute, in a horrible way, but I'm staying in my spacesuit probably forever."

"What's up?" called Moe on the intercom from the control room. "Can anybody hear me?"

"Bruiser sniffed a pod," said Uhuru. "He's wearing an alien for a hat."

"What?" asked Moe. "Have you lost your brains too? I should have put on a spacesuit. I'm doomed."

"Time is of the essence," said Caine. "Let's get them up to the laboratory. Uhuru, you might want to work on the plumbing while we conduct our scientific business. The air is rather thick in here."

Caine's laboratory was just off the okra room, and they had to move several plants off the potting bench to make enough room to stretch Bruiser out.

"Shouldn't we start with Christianson?" asked Tootsie. "I mean, if we make a mistake I'd rather it was him. Bruiser's no prize, but . . ."

"Sentimentality has no place in the objective world of science," said Caine. "It leads to muddled thinking and erroneous conclusions. We start with Bruiser. Pass me the trowel."

"Trowel?" asked Bill.

"On the magnetboard there, between the rake and the hoe," said Caine. "As an ex-farmboy, I'm sure you have the residual wit to recognize a trowel."

"But this is a time for quick-thinking medical action," complained Bill, nonetheless passing Caine the trowel.

"Exactly what I have in mind," said Caine. "I want to see if I can pry this attached alien off of Bruiser."

"Be gentle," said Tootsie.

"I can assure you I won't harm Bruiser," said Caine, trying to pry loose a cute little webbed foot.

"I was thinking more of the alien," said Tootsie. "Even though it's probably really dangerous and could kill us all, it's adorable."

"More sentimentality," grumped Caine, laying down the trowel in frustration. "It won't let go. Pass me the pruning shears, Bill."

"Are you going to cut it off?" shouted a horrified Larry. Or Curly.

"No, I want a blood sample."

"I wouldn't do that," said Rambette hastily. "We don't know anything at all about its blood. It could be caustic and the slightest drop might eat its way through the floor and all the other decks below us until it breached the hull and we all died."

"Shut up," he implied. "It's Bruiser's blood I need to sample."

"Oh, that's different," said Rambette. "Take all you want."

"Thanks," Caine said dryly, clipping off the tiniest

tip of Bruiser's left earlobe and collecting a few drops of blood in a small clay flower pot. "I'll just run this through my analyzer."

"I'm impressed," said Tootsie. "I've never seen real science in action."

Bill looked at the pruning shears and wondered if he could borrow them when Caine was through. He'd broken two of Rambette's knives trying unsuccessfully to clip the toenails on his elephant foot, and she refused to loan him any more.

"Amazing," said Caine, punching buttons on his analyzer.

"What did you find?" asked Bill, as the crew gathered around Caine.

"A total lack of chlorophyll," he said. "I've never seen anything like it."

"We *are* talking human beings here," said Bill. "While Bruiser certainly has his faults, he's probably just a little more animal than vegetable."

"This is the first time I've run anything but plant stems or crushed-up leaves through here," said Caine, shaking his head. "I *always* get chlorophyll."

"Where me be?" asked Bruiser, sitting up. "What's for dinner? I'm starved."

"Me too," said Christianson. "I've never been as hungry as I am now."

"You're both alive!" cried Bill.

"What else? You nuts?" grumbled Bruiser, holding a now-limp alien in his hand. "What's dis thing? Last I remember I was sniffing a pod."

"Easy with that!" yelled Caine, rushing over and grabbing it away from Bruiser. "That's a valuable alien creature."

"I got one too," said Christianson, holding it out

at arm's length by a limp webbed foot. "But I think mine is dead."

"They're both dead," said Caine. "How do you feel, Bruiser?"

"Real hungry," he said. "Besides dat, I feel good— except maybe I got kinda pain in my earlobe. Let's eat."

"They've been through a lot," said Rambette. "And I'm starved myself."

"I shall stay here and examine the aliens," said Caine. "A true scientist ignores such mundane concerns as food while hot on the trail of unprecedented and electrifying discoveries."

"Chow time. Let's go," Bruiser said salivatingly.

"What's that crappy odor?" sniffed Christianson as they started heading for the galley.

"Don't ask," said Bill, relieved to be free of aliens and back to the normal concerns of plumbing problems and good food.

"Look!" said Tootsie. "Oh, it's gone."

"What's gone?"

"I thought I saw a mouse. It scuttled around a corner before I could get a good look at it."

"Better be porkuswine chops left or dere be trouble," said Bruiser.

Scuttled? Bill thought. *Did she really say scuttled?*

CHAPTER 10

THERE WERE INDEED PORKUSWINE CHOPS left, at least, there were until about ten seconds after Bruiser sat down. It wouldn't have taken him even that long except he had to stab his fork into the back of Christianson's hand to make sure he got them all.

Bruiser and Christianson were putting down the food as fast as it appeared on the table. They both had been known to have well above average appetites, but this was ridiculous.

"This is ridiculous," said Rambette, holding up a limp piece of chicken-fried sea slug. "Tell me, is this supposed to be crisp?"

"What you see is what you get," said Uhuru, who was seated at the large table, still wearing his space-suit. "Fresh from the microwave."

"You can't microwave sea slug," said Tootsie. "It's supposed to be crispy. You've got to use a deep fryer."

"The fryer broke when we landed," said Uhuru.

"It was a brave little fryer, but it's junk now. Boy, those rattlesnake caviar blintzes look good."

"They're delicious," said Christianson, grabbing a handful and pouring half a bottle of hot sauce on them. "You better dig in right now if you want some. I can't control myself."

"I'm not getting out of this suit," whined Uhuru. "Being turned into a zombie doesn't appeal to me."

"Dat zombie stuff is just Caine's stupid idea," said Bruiser, pulling all four drumsticks off a roasted Procyon-3 turkey. "Jus' look at me. Normal like always. Pass some more of dat fou-fou."

"On the way," whined Captain Blight, who had been assigned kitchen duty and was really chained to the stove. "I'm toasting the fou-fou now. You can't expect me to do everything at once."

"I'm finishing this one, so I'll have another soylent greenburger too!" said Christianson, bolting the last mouthful then licking his fingers enthusiastically. "I think that dehydrated reconstituted chipped spider-burgers are the best thing in the galaxy. But I'll settle for second best. You sure you don't want some, Uhuru?"

Bill could hear Uhuru's stomach growling frantically as the man stared longingly at the sizzling pan of frying burgers that emitted a luscious green smoke. He reached down beside him and patted Barfer on the head. The dog was happily munching on some okra he'd dug out of the garden.

"Which one of you is Moe?" Bill asked. The three clones were sitting across from him gnawing enthusiastically on broasted archeopteryx wings.

"Him. The knucklehead hogging the lortsauce."

"What do we need to get us going, Moe?" asked Bill, nibbling a bit of blintz.

"Besides the tape? Some coils of baling wire would help patch things together. And, let's see, steel plates for the bulkheads, screens for the shields, and fuses; we're real short on fuses. We've got all kinds of welding equipment and miscellaneous supplies in the repair bays, but it'll take time."

"Time is the one thing we don't have," said Bill. "But I *do* know fuses. I have a Fusetender's Mate Fourth Class rating so I'll take care of that."

"I can do the bulkheads," said Bruiser between gulps. "But I'll need a hand getting the steel plates out of the station."

"Not me," said Tootsie. "I'm not going back into that terrible place. Pass the fou-fou."

"I can't take it!" cried Uhuru, removing his helmet and seizing up a broasted archeopteryx wing two meters long. "I know I'll regret this, but I'm like starving to death."

"You ought to try chewing your food, Bruiser," said Rambette. "Goes down easier that way."

"Chewing slow Bruiser down," he sputtered around a mouthful of food. "Is waste of eating time."

"Here's your burger," said Captain Blight. "Rare. The black bits are spider chitin."

"Yuck," moaned Tootsie. "I'll never eat a spider again after the way you cook them."

"*HEY!*" bellowed Bruiser.

The dinner conversation stopped cold in its tracks. Everybody froze. Even Barfer quit munching on his okra and stared at the big man.

"*HEY!*" he cried, slapping the side of his head. "I t'ink I'm losing my mind!"

"I knew it," wailed Uhuru. "I should never have come out of my spacesuit. There goes my common sense, and here comes zombiedom."

"Where's my Slasher?" Bruiser roared. "What bowb stole my axe?"

"Cool it," Bill cozened. "Nobody—"

"Don't you tell what to do, you bowbheaded MP," snarled Bruiser. "It's all your fault."

"My fault?"

"It's still down dere—in the pod cavern. Larry said he carry it back."

"Me? Come off it, Curly. *You* were supposed get it."

"Somebody's got to get it," Bruiser growled. "I t'ink it's MP's job."

"Me?" asked Bill.

"You got maybe some kinda ear trouble?" barked Bruiser. "If your big-stoop foot hadn't knocked hole in floor none of dis would have happened. Now, get your chunk down hole and get my Slasher—or I get it myself, come back and use axe on you. You no have to worry about your foot no more. You catch on?"

"I think I got the picture," said Bill.

"Good," grunted Bruiser with a satisfiedly sadistic smile. "Now dat settled, we finish dis meal. Who's got rest of blintzes?"

"More here, sir," said a disgusted Captain Blight. "They're just the way you like them."

While Bruiser and Christianson were dividing up a gigantic pile of half-raw rattlesnake caviar blintzes Caine walked in. He was carrying one of the dead aliens and looked worried.

"We have a problem," he said.

"I know," said Uhuru, noshing away. "Bruiser lost his axe and—*hey!*—get that thing out of here!"

"It is merely a discarded integument," said Caine. "It's no danger whatsoever."

S T O P   R E A D I N G !

AT LEAST FOR A FEW MINUTES. THIS WARNING
is for your own good, really. It has been proven by
exhaustive laboratory tests that continuous reading,
without taking a break, causes eyestrain and bladder
trouble. That's it. Get up. Stretch. Yawn, you relaxed
devil, you! Then go to the little boy's room (or the little
girl's room, depending on your sex or voyeuristic
vagaries.) Then settle back down with this unputdown-
able book.

AND LOOK—

at what your friendly editor has arranged for your
edification and pleasure. A portfolio of artwork that will
give you incredible insight into the intricacies of interest
in this volume—not to mention a good look at Bill's
tusks.

ARE YOU READY?

Then turn the page . . .

Note the interesting number of toes on the stone foot. An instant after this was taken the camera was junk. The cameraman is still in the hospital.

The okra beds in full bloom. Bill not sure if he wants to eat it or walk on it.

Just good friends. Rambette and Bruiser. You can't see it, but the nearest knife handle is engraved SWAK.

Captain Blight is immensely proud of his Okra
Awards—if not his table manners.

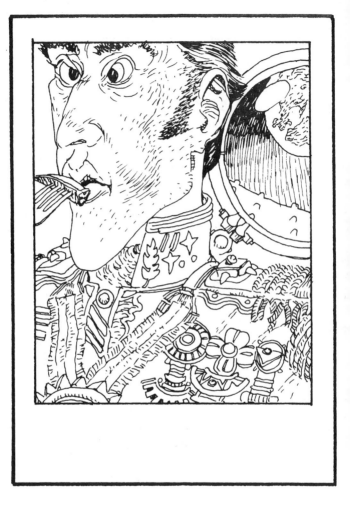

Mr. Christianson actually likes okra; he is the numbnuts of gastronomy.

Larry, Moe and Curly are identical clones. It is impossible to tell them apart. PS—who wants to?

A singularly repulsive photo of Uhuru and Tootsie. A replacement lens was needed for the camera since this pic cracked the old one.

Bill shrieks in fear when attacked by repulsive alien. Which turns out to be Barfer the dog. Which isn't much better.

Through the docking tube. A situation very much like a digestive stroll through a gargantuan intenstine.

Don't look at this—but if you must, see the mummies' bones just turn to dust!

Some are born dumb: some have stupidity thrust upon them: some attain moronity. Mr. Christianson—who pokes a pod!—succeeds in all three categories.

Bruiser getting zombified by a cute lil' alien. He's the only one not smiling.

From bad to worse. Analysis of a scuttling alien reveals
the fact that it is pretty repulsive.

Eager Beager attempts—with very little success—to communicate intelligently with Bill at his mentally feeblest.

Close encounters of the forklift kind.

"A what?" said Rambette. "It's not nearly so cute now that it's a dead whatever you called it."

"Integument is the scientific word for skin," said Caine. "It shed its skin like a snake. I was halfway through the autopsy when I discovered it was empty inside. Bruiser was right, it's nothing but fur and feathers."

"This is hardly proper dinner conversation," complained Christianson, though he did not stop eating.

"You, of all people, should be paying attention, Mr. Christianson," said Caine. "It wouldn't hurt for Bruiser to listen up, either."

"Me listen good," mumbled the big man as he cracked the archeopteryx bones with his teeth and noisily sucked out the marrow.

"This isn't going to be pretty," lectured Caine. "But science—being hard, cold, and objective—often isn't. Pretty might be said to be a luxury that scientific research can't afford."

"Gee, I'm impressed," said Rambette unimpressedly. "Slide those latkes over here."

"Dey good, huh?" asked Bruiser. "Though me feel sorry for all da rattlesnakes."

"Don't bother," said Tootsie. "They died in a good cause. Indigestion."

"Would you people kindly listen?" Caine snapped surlily. "I have deduced that we are dealing with the larval form of an extremely complex creature." He waved the alien skin to make his point, and a webbed foot fell into the salad. Bruiser picked it out and threw it on the floor. Barfer sniffed it, growled unhappily, and went back to his okra.

"We had firsthand observation of the egg hatchery," he continued. "That's a good place to start examining the beast's life cycle. After an appropriate incubation period they apparently hatch and wait to attach themselves to any living forms that are handy."

"This is spoiling my appetite," moaned Tootsie.

"Not mine," Bruiser said happily. "Who got da chopped onions?"

"Whereupon they gather nutrients, pass into a dormant stage, and molt."

"Wait a minute there," said Christianson, watching the captain throw bits of battered sea slug into the simmering oil. "I don't think I like that *gathering nutrients* part. Are you trying to tell me it was sucking my blood?"

"Something like that," said Caine. "But I wouldn't worry about *that* part. They're pretty small at that point in their life cycle, so they probably don't require much in the way of nutrition. Just a little blood. You can easily spare it. The only complication would be that you might feel a little hungrier than usual afterwards."

"I haven't noticed anything like that," said Christianson, chomping half of a spiderburger in one bite.

"Me either," said Bruiser, dipping his tenth turkey leg into the hot sauce.

"Bloodsucking aliens?" mused Rambette. "Could they possibly be galactic vampires?"

"First we had mummies," moaned Tootsie. "Next we had zombies and now we've got vampires. We've had every damned monster in the book."

"I think we're missing trolls," suggested Bill helpfully. "And dragons."

"Don't forget werewolves," said Rambette.

"Maybe they're next," quavered Tootsie.

"That's hard to predict," Caine said. "But one thing we can be reasonably sure of is that whatever form it takes next, it won't be little and cute anymore. It's outgrown that stage."

"That's cheerful news," said Bill, poking his finger into his midriff to see if he could stow any more chow away.

"So where are they?" asked Uhuru. "If they molted, where did they go off to? They better not be loose on the ship."

"That's a very real possibility," said the android science officer. "And there may not be two anymore. There may be four."

"Four?" asked Larry or Curly or Moe, stealing a latke off another clone's plate. "How come four?"

"They could have divided. Lots of creatures do that. Amoebas, for instance. But that's not the bad news."

"Wait up," said Bill, "We got maybe four vampires loose on the ship, and that's not the bad news? What could be worse?"

"It's quite possible they are not running around on the ship."

"That's a relief," said Uhuru.

"No, it's not," said Caine slowly. "That's the bad news. They might be developing to their next stage inside the bodies of Bruiser and Mr. Christianson."

Everybody but the two aforementioned possible hosts stopped eating and stared in horror at the potential danger in their midst.

"Dat's not funny," said Bruiser, glowering around at the horrified spectators. "I never heard of nothin' like dat."

"It's really quite common in nature," cozened Caine. "All of us totally competent scientists know of many examples. Wasps that lay their eggs on caterpillars are the ones I'm most familiar with. But, of course, there are tapeworms and all kinds of other parasites."

"I hear that people with tapeworms have big appetites," said Bill, eyeballing Bruiser suspiciously.

"There is certain evidence to justify that supposition," admitted Caine.

Bruiser and Christianson were the only two still eating. Everyone else's appetites had been ruined by the tapeworm talk and a growing certainty that something awful was about to happen.

"If that's true," said Uhuru, not taking his eyes off Bruiser, "what happens next?"

"When the alien reaches the next stage of its development it—or they—will come out."

"How?" asked Bill, filled with mounting dread.

"Any way they want to," said Caine.

"Ugh!" gasped Bruiser, clutching his stomach. "Urp! Ack! Bletch!"

"What's happening?" screamed Uhuru, pushing his chair back and jumping away from the table.

"We're all going to die," moaned Tootsie. "I knew it!"

"Urp! Urp!" coughed Bruiser. "Ack!"

"He's having a fit!" cried a clone. "Somebody do something! Put a spoon in his mouth!"

"I think he's choking," said Bill. "If he is, putting a spoon in his mouth would be a bad idea."

"The aliens are trying to bust out of his body in a bloody nasty horrible way!" moaned Tootsie. "We're all going to die!"

"How interesting," said Caine. "I really should be taking notes. This could be of considerable interest to the scientific community."

"Garp!" garped Bruiser, flopping back in his chair. "Ick! Urp!"

"We've got to do something," said Rambette. "Bill, you can't sit there and let him die!"

"I'm thinking it over," said Bill. "He wants to chop off my legs, you know."

"Nobody's perfect," said Rambette, pounding Bruiser on the back. "Give me a hand."

"I think you're supposed to grab him around the waist and give a hard jerk," said Bill, getting up.

"So do it!" shrieked Rambette. "We don't have much time!"

"I can't get my arms around him," said Bill. "He's too fat."

Rambette and Bill joined hands, and after arguing about the possible location of Bruiser's diaphragm, gave a solid jerk. Bruiser grunted loudly and the table was suddenly splattered heavily.

"Yeow!" screamed Tootsie. "We're as good as dead!"

"It's a ghastly mess," cried Uhuru, sneaking toward the door. "I knew I shouldn't have let you back on the ship. Anybody see the aliens?"

"There's nothing here but partially digested food," said Caine, poking around with androidal scientific curiosity. "He was simply choking. That's most disappointing. I was hoping for an alien."

"I told him to chew his food better," said Rambette. "But would he listen? No."

"Anyone for seconds?" asked Captain Blight, wheeling in a cart overloaded with food. He screamed when they all started to punch him. "What are you doing? What's happening? And if you have complaints—so do I. I was stirring up another batch of blintzes and—*hey!*—somebody get that mouse scuttling across the floor. We can't have any rodents in the dining area."

Bill stomped down hard with his elephant foot. What crunched underneath didn't feel much like a mouse. He lifted his foot slowly and looked at what was stuck to the sole with horror.

"Did you get it?" asked Blight.

"I certainly did," said Bill. "But I don't think it was a mouse. Come look."

"Fascinating," said Caine, as everybody gathered around to examine Bill's foot.

"Is that one of the aliens?" moaned Tootsie.

"It *was* one," Caine said. "Bill has, unfortunately, squashed it beyond recognition. I would have liked to examine it."

"Where's it come from?" asked Tootsie. "Did it come busting out of Bruiser?"

"No," said Blight. "It came busting out of the kitchen. I saw it scuttle out from behind a sack of flour."

"Are those teeth?" asked Rambette. "Those white things stuck in the middle of all that gore?"

"They look like teeth to me," Christianson said. "Pretty sharp ones, too."

"Sure are a lot of them," said Rambette. "A *whole* lot of them."

CHAPTER 11

"I BELIEVE THAT IT IS FAIRLY SAFE TO SAY we're not dealing with a vegetarian here," said Caine, examining the remains of the alien with his pocket electronic magnifying microscope and throat spray. "These are the sharpest teeth I've ever seen."

"You saved my life," said Bruiser, giving Bill a bone-crushing bear hug. "I owe you one."

"Gasp," gasped Bill. "Gasp."

"You good guy. So I go with you back down into dat dark place to get my Slasher."

"Thanks," croaked Bill.

"I would not advise returning to the station," advised Caine. "Much less paying a visit to the basement. It could be quite hazardous."

"But we need supplies from there or we won't be able to get off this crappy planet," cried Uhuru. "Somebody's got to go back."

"That somebody is *not* going to be me," moaned Tootsie.

"Quit all that moaning, Tootsie," Rambette commanded sneeringly. "It's getting on my nerves."

"Would you rather I whined?" she whined.

"No, go back to moaning," shuddered Rambette. "Whining drives me up the wall. Moaning just gets on my nerves."

"Back off a little," said Uhuru. "We're all under a great deal of stress. Everybody would feel a lot better if we all took a brief time-out to get our alpha rhythms in order. Let's just stop and smell the roses."

"Shove your alpha rhythms," snapped Rambette. "I don't believe in that ancient new age stuff."

"I don't know about anybody else," muttered Bill, "but I could use some sleep."

"Sleep?" screeched Uhuru. "How can you think of sleep at a time like this?"

"Easy," yawned Bill. "Have you noticed that none of us have had any sleep since we landed on this planet? How long have we been here? Weeks?"

"More like days," yawned Tootsie. "Long enough. Too long."

"You got it in one," said Bill. "And the latrine. I haven't noticed anybody trotting off to the head either."

"Something wrong with your nose?" Rambette sniffed. "I wouldn't go there for anything. The compost pile smells better than that place."

"I been twice," belched Bruiser. "No problem."

"You humans had better get some rest," suggested Caine. "I will stay awake examining what remains of the squashed creature."

"What if the alien vampires come up and suck us dry while we sleep?" Tootsie shuddered. "I don't want to be turned into a mummy or a zombie, not even a troll."

"I will keep watch," said Caine. "Androids do not need sleep in the sense that humans do. We doze a little while our batteries are recharging, but that's all."

"How are your batteries?" asked Uhuru anxiously.

"My batteries are fine, thank you," said Caine testily. "I suggest you all retire to your bunks and catch up with what you call sack-time. I will keep watch for the vampire aliens."

"Did anyone close the door to the docking tube?" asked Uhuru. "We don't need any more of those alien creatures in the ship."

"Larry did," said Curly or Moe. "I saw him myself."

"I guess it's okay, then," said Uhuru. "But I'm leaving a night-light on, and I'm sleeping in my spacesuit."

"Big coward," said Bruiser. "Come, Bill. Get stinking dog and let's go."

Barfer growled and snarled outside the door to Bill's bunk, but a search revealed nothing more sinister than Bruiser's dirty magazines. Bill decided to leave his night-light on and Bruiser muttered sadistic stories about his adventures with Slasher until he fell asleep.

But when sleep came, it was a troubled and disturbed sleep, filled with horrible nightmares of the creeping and crawling variety. At one point, Bill thought he felt something scuttling over his body and sucking blood out of his neck. Then he dreamed he was lurching around the corridors of the ship bumping into things, a vacant expression in his eyes and his arms held straight out like a zombie.

"Wake up Bill," said Caine, shaking him by the shoulders. "You've been sleepwalking."

"Where am I?" Bill asked, confused.

"You're in the okra room, and the plants are in one of their night cycles. I found you lurching around in the dark bumping into things like a zombie."

"A zombie! I had a bad dream."

"You had more than that," said Caine. "Look at your neck."

"I can't," said Bill.

"Come on, it's not that bad."

"No. I can't see my neck without a mirror. It's like looking in my ear. I just can't do it. What's wrong?"

"I can't be sure here in the darkness," murmured Caine. "But it looks like there are two little blood-encrusted pinpricks on your neck. Let's go back to my laboratory, the light's better there."

"Maybe," Bill said hesitantly. "But no blood samples."

"If you insist."

They were met in the laboratory by Rambette, Tootsie, and Uhuru, who all said that they had been unable to sleep. Uhuru was once again wearing his spacesuit and had hung a string of garlic cloves around his neck.

"Bill looks pale," gasped Rambette. "What's wrong?"

"It would appear to this educated observer that an alien has been feeding upon him," said Caine, moving close to Bill and taking a good look at his neck. "This is most interesting from a clinical standpoint. How do you feel?"

"I feel like I've been lurching around in the dark bumping into stuff," said Bill. "Aside from a few bruises, I'm okay. Just a little drained."

"I knew it!" moaned Tootsie. "They're going to

pick us off one by one. I thought you were going to keep watch, Caine."

"I only dozed off once," said the android. "Scientific investigation is a most strenuous activity."

"Look what I found by Bill's bunk," said Bruiser, coming into the room holding a fuzzy object. "We got to get my Slasher right away."

"What is it?" wailed Tootsie.

"Another shed skin," Caine said, taking it from Bruiser and spreading it out on his potting bench. "Evidently the creature molted again after it had drinkies from Bill. You can see it is much larger than the one he unfortunately stomped."

"Uglier, too," said Rambette, poking it with one of her knives. "And even more horrendous, if that's possible."

The molted skin was about the size of a large dog. It was clear from the remains that the alien at this stage of development was mostly teeth, fangs, and claws. It had a huge, sloping head and a spiked tail as long as one of Bill's right arms. Everything was covered with a thick coat of orange hair and purple warts.

"That looks real dangerous, not to mention disgusting," said Uhuru, adjusting his garlic necklace. "A monster that size could do serious damage to a person."

"Don't forget that its dimensions have increased beyond what we see here," said Caine. "The alien shed its skin because it grew out of it, and therefore in all probability it is now quite gigantic. My scientific curiosity is aroused. I wonder what its maximum size will be? It is possible there is no limit to its growth as long as its food supply holds out."

"I don't think that I like being called a food supply," complained Bill.

"Everyone here is a potential food supply," said Caine. "Except, of course, for myself. I seriously doubt that these creatures would find androids a suitable source of nutrition."

"Well, I ain't gonna be no lunch for no monster," said Bruiser.

"And that goes double for me," said Uhuru.

"You egocentric humans fail to grasp the far-reaching implications of our extraordinary discovery," sniffed Caine, inspecting a dangling leg. "We have an incredibly adaptable organism here, one that can assume many different shapes and forms."

"These horrors *do* come in all sizes," said Rambette. "As near as I can see, they tend to lean more toward large and larger. They all give me the creeps, except when they were little and cute."

"The aliens must be viewed as an opportunity to advance the body of mankind's knowledge," Caine said. "Each stage of development is fascinating in its own right and should be studied down to its last molecule."

"You'd feel differently if you were sitting on an alien's plate," said Tootsie.

"I rather doubt that," said Caine dryly, measuring the carcass with a yardstick and taking notes in a small book. "I am an objective observer at all times."

"I observe you're getting alien gunk all over that yardstick," said Rambette. "And some of it is dripping on your shoe."

"I shall be famous," said Caine. "This will make a wonderful research paper. I'll be published in all the best journals. As a botanist I faced a long and boring future, but the future's not what it used to be anymore. Everything has changed. As a researcher specializing in disgusting aliens, I'll be known across the universe. I'll be the number one expert. I'll—*hey!*—who stole my fur and feathers? They were right here a little while ago."

"Maybe they walked away," said Tootsie.

"This is no time for levity," snapped Caine. "This is serious business. We must compare the chemical makeup of the different stages from which we have samples. Where are the scrapings I took from Bill's foot? Has everything disappeared?"

"Maybe you're turning into an absentminded professor," suggested Rambette.

"Everybody help me, look around," ordered Caine. "I must find my samples."

Reluctantly, the crew started opening drawers and peering behind potted plants and bags of fertilizer. Only Uhuru refused to join in the hunt, saying he wasn't going to have anything to do with the horrifying aliens, science or no science.

"Lose something?" asked Captain Blight as he walked into the room with Mr. Christianson.

"My samples," said Caine. "I must find them."

"Oh, that old junk? I threw it all on the compost pile."

"You what?"

"My plants have to live, too," Blight said haughtily. "We can't let the okra die just because we're busy fighting aliens."

"Those were valuable scientific specimens," snapped Caine.

"They're compost now," Christianson observed. "We just finished turning the pile."

"My career is in tatters," Caine whined. "We must

get more samples. Everybody go back to sleep. I'll keep watch and try to catch an alien when it comes to feed."

"Do I look like bait?" Rambette asked angrily.

"I'm never sleeping again," moaned Tootsie.

"Bill and me gonna get Slasher," said Bruiser. "When I sleep is gonna be wit da axe at side in bed."

"Getting Slasher back is a good idea," Caine said quickly. "And while you're down there in the cavern, why don't you sniff a pod or two. I wasn't finished with the fur and feathers."

"I ain't sniffing no pods or nothin'!" roared Bruiser. "Bill, he can maybe do dat."

"If you want pods, get them yourself," Bill snapped. "I'm officially retiring from the pod-gathering business as of right now."

"I vote for getting the ship out of here as soon as possible, if not sooner," said Uhuru. "I've got a list of stuff we need from the station. While you're down there dodging aliens and facing certain death, you might as well pick up a few things for me."

"Do I detect a slight reluctance on your part to leave the ship, Uhuru?" asked Rambette. "It couldn't be that you're turning coward on us?"

"Not me," said Uhuru. "I simply thought it would be a more efficient use of our resources if I stayed here and supervised repairs while you all did the gathering. Someone has to be in charge, you know. Otherwise we won't get anything done."

"Watch out for that mantle of responsibility stuff," said Blight. "Once you put it on, it's hard to drop it."

"I'll take that chance," sniffed Uhuru.

"Who elected you to be boss of the repair operation, anyway?" asked Tootsie. "I don't remember casting my ballot. Curly and Bill both know this ship better than you do."

"We can draw straws," said Uhuru hopefully. "I just happen to have some plastic tubing that would do."

"Forget your straws," said Rambette. "What we need to do first is—"

"Curly!" cried two of the clones as they charged into the room. "An alien took Curly!"

C H A P T E R **12**

"CALM DOWN, IF YOU CAN," CAINE AD-
vised the extremely agitated clones. "What did he
look like?"

"Curly? He looks just like Moe and me, only a
whole lot uglier. You know what Curly looks like."

"No. The alien. What did the alien look like?"

"The usual. All hairy, bumpy, ugly. Lots of teeth.
A funny tail."

"How big was it?"

"Bigger than Curly. Uglier, too."

"It's still growing," said Caine. "I do wish you
would give me a more detailed description. I can
hardly write 'a funny tail' in my journal."

"Listen, bowb, we've got to get Curly back,"
snapped Bill. "Curly first, research later."

"That's right," said Tootsie. "We can't let the aliens
eat Curly or suck all the life force out of him and turn
him into a mummy."

"That's real compassionate of you, Bill," said Rambette. "I didn't think you had it in you."

"I don't," admitted Bill. "I was actually more concerned about the fact that he's the only one who knows how to fix the autopilot."

"Clear thinking," said Blight. "I slept through that part in officer's school."

"They don't teach autopilot repair anymore," said Christianson. "It's too complicated for us officers. If we had to learn stuff like that we wouldn't have time to learn the real important things like how to give lavish parties, raise our sperm count, and brutalize the troops. And, if I might be so bold as to suggest it, the MP should bring that stinking dog. It might help; maybe Barfer can sniff out a trail."

"He's probably stuffing his face in the okra room," said Bill. "Where else would he be?"

Sure enough, Barfer was chowing down on some *Abelmoschus humungous,* happily stumbling from one end of the bed to the other, picking out only the tenderest, tastiest buds. Blight was about to kill the grazing dog but was convinced not to when Caine informed him that a selective harvest would stimulate new growth in the established plants and was, indeed, a recommended procedure.

They picked up the trail outside Curly's door. It was not a terribly difficult trail to follow, being a strip of shedded orange fur a yard wide going down the corridor. It led them to what used to be the door to the docking tube.

The door was a twisted and destroyed wreck, lying in pieces on the floor. All the edges were melted, as if they had been sizzled by a giant welding torch or hosed down by a caustic acid.

"This is awful," said Uhuru, scribbling on a piece

of paper. "I'll have to revise my shopping list. Pick me up a door if you find one."

"Such power," said Caine admiringly, hefting a chunk of broken door. "They are truly amazing creatures."

"They're creeping horrors, if you ask me," shivered Rambette. "Let's find Curly and get the damn ship ready to go. If you want to study them, do it on your own time."

The station appeared just as they had left it, except for about a thousand crisscrossing orange fur trails of all sizes. The crew huddled together in the command center.

"We've got to split up into groups," said Bill, tearing Uhuru's shopping list into strips and giving everyone a piece. "This place is too large to explore as one unit. You'll each take a list and find the items on it. But be careful about wandering off on your own—it might have a negative impact on your life."

"Look at all these fur tracks," moaned Tootsie. "There must be hundreds of these creatures up and about. I don't think even being here is a good idea. I mean, what if the creatures already had Curly for lunch? We ought to just fix the ship and get off this miserable planet."

"Our first objective is to find our shipmate Curly," said Bill, assuming his best Trooper stance. "Not only is he our good buddy—but we can't fly the ship without him, so fixing the ship won't help much. Our second objective is to find the material Uhuru needs for repairs."

"Our third objective is to gather specimens," said Caine. "Remember, scientific observation should never be curtailed, even if we are currently fighting for our very lives."

"You want specimens?" asked Bruiser. "Then you come to da basement wit me and Bill? Plenty action dere, you bet."

"I'm sticking with Rambette," said Captain Blight. "She's armed to the teeth."

"I made a flamethrower out of a welding torch," said Larry or Moe happily. "If I see anything move that isn't one of us, I'm going to fry it on the spot."

"I wish I had big chainsaw," said Bruiser. "I'd massacre dem Texas-style like in da video."

"What's a Texas?" asked Rambette.

"What's a chainsaw?" asked Christianson.

"I think Texas is a star," said Blight.

"A double star?" asked Bill.

"No, a lone star," said Blight.

"Shut up!" Rambette shouted. "Every minute we stand around jawing about the situation is a minute more they have to munch on Curly. I think we've been breathing spores again."

The rope was still tied to the heavy desk, and Bill followed Bruiser down into the threatening unknown with a great deal of trepidation. Not to mention fear. And trembling. Caine followed Bill, happy to be in search of specimens and secure in the knowledge that androids were unpalatable to alien taste buds. Barfer once again drew guard duty at the top of the rope.

"I wish I had that flamethrower instead of this flashlight," Bill complained as they looked around. "It's a great flashlight and all that, but if I'm attacked. . . . Flamethrowers are better."

"All we need is Slasher," grinned Bruiser threateningly. "I'm going to wander off in da dark by myself and find my axe."

"Look over here," said Caine. "This is most interesting."

"What did you find?" asked Bill, going towards the light of Caine's flashlight as Bruiser wandered off alone.

"Look at these pods," he said. "Most of the ones in this pool have hatched. There must be a whole horde of the little monsters around here somewhere. Maybe I can collect a few live specimens. I know that I'd feel bad if one wrapped itself around your head and maybe killed you, but consider for a moment the incredible value that would hold for the advancement of scientific knowledge."

"I'm considering," said Bill. "Considering that I would like to suck your brain out through your nose and examine it to see where ideas like that come from."

"Yes, well, I can see your point. But look—some of these pods are in the process of hatching. Take a close look at this one."

"I'll pass, if you don't mind."

"It's glowing with an eerie light," said Caine, scribbling frantically in his notebook with his flashlight tucked in his armpit. "It's moving. Shift your light this way so I can get a closer look."

"That's maybe not the galaxy's greatest idea," said Bill.

"Don't be ridiculous. I must proceed with my observations. I am immune to the—"

"Watch out!" cried Bill as the pod split open and a creature popped out.

"Yow!" Caine screamed, swinging at the alien with his flashlight. "That hurt!"

"Keep it down," called Bruiser. "You're making enough noise to wake da dead."

Together Bill and Caine beat on the cute little baby monster until it quit moving.

"Good thing it's so dark in here," said Bill. "If I was able to see good, I would never have been able to kill such a cute little thing. You'd be one dead android."

"I don't understand," said Caine, shaking. "I was *sure* they wouldn't attack me. I must have misjudged their adaptability."

"You want to take this carcass?" asked Bill, playing his light on the squashed pile of fur and feathers, already feeling guilty for dispatching the cute little critter. "Maybe study it a little bit?"

"No thanks," said Caine. "It tried to kill me. Something this deadly should be eradicated from the face of the universe, not put in zoos or laboratories where they might escape and wreak all kinds of havoc."

"Yow!" hooted Bruiser. "Yow! Yow!"

"Are you all right?" cried Bill. "Did an alien jump out and get you?"

"No," called Bruiser. "I found Slasher."

"Great," said Caine, heading for the rope in a real big hurry. "It's time to make our retreat. If Curly's down here, there's no hope for him."

"Wait up!" cried Bruiser. "Dere's a whole flock of dose cute little deadly beasties flying around me. Good t'ing it dark and I can chop dem up with Slasher without feeling bad."

Caine was already halfway up the rope, kicking and beating at the swarm of flying fur and feathers that surrounded him. Spurred on by a sudden shot of adrenalin, Bill caught up with him in an instant. Together they scampered up the rope to the hole where Barfer was keeping the critters at bay, growling and snarling and snapping as if someone was trying to steal his okra.

"Get that mattress," said Bill as he and Caine crawled out of the hole. "As soon as Bruiser gets here, we'll cover up that gateway to hell."

"Dat was close," said Bruiser, popping up and helping tilt the desk on top of the mattress. "Dey almost got me."

"Good dog," said Bill, patting Barfer on the head.

"Did you find Curly?" asked Rambette, walking into the room with Captain Blight and Christianson.

"No, but dat place is crawling with fur and feathers," said Bruiser. "Dey're all over da place."

"We've had our own problems up here," said Blight. "Better watch your step."

"It's the scuttling ones we've got attacking us," said Christianson. "Like the one that Bill stomped. Must be hundreds of them up here."

"They look like little crabs up close," said Rambette. "Got a touch of mouse about them too. They can hurt you bad. Look at Blight's ankle."

The captain's pant leg was shredded and he had a bloody bandage wrapped around his ankle. Christianson's boots were scarred from a few near-misses.

"You won't have any trouble getting specimens here," Rambette said to Caine. "All you have to do is stand still for a couple of minutes."

"I'm through gathering samples for the time being, thank you," sniffed the android. "Maybe I wasn't designed to be on the cutting edge of scientific investigation. There's a lot to be said about working with plants. Plants stay where you put them and most of them don't leap up and attack you."

"We got everything on our part of the shopping list," said Blight. "But no sign of Curly. I wish I hadn't slept through autopilot repair, but it's too late to go back and rectify that little mistake. No sense in feeling bad about something I can't change."

"This is a huge place," said Christianson. "Curly could be anywhere. It might take weeks or months to explore every dangerously dark corner, especially dodging loathsome aliens all the time. We'll probably die before we find him."

"The more we kill, the more they keep on coming," said Blight. "We're fighting a losing battle against impossible odds. And to think, all this is a result of my sweet tooth. I wish I hadn't hoarded all the doughnuts. It probably wasn't a very good thing to do, but what's done is done."

"While you're busy repenting," said Rambette, "don't forget to feel sorry about not letting us have any water."

"That too," groaned Blight.

An alien crab-mouse critter scuttled across the floor. Bill stomped it with his elephant foot before he even had a chance to realize what he was doing.

"Good show," said Christianson. "That foot may be huge and ugly, but it sure stomps aliens."

"That's very odd," said Bill, scraping the gore off the bottom of his foot. "My foot seems to have a mind of its own. It stomps before I tell it to."

"If we weren't in such mortal danger, it would be interesting to explore that phenomenon," said Caine. "Perhaps it is some sort of a genetic memory. I seem to recall that elephants were very fond of stomping on mice. Of course, since our very lives are on the line, we will have to postpone any investigation until a later date, and simply be thankful for your quick reactions."

Bill stomped another alien.

"This way," shouted Tootsie from the door. "Everybody follow me. We've found what's left of Curly."

CHAPTER 13

"WATCH YOUR STEP," CRIED TOOTSIE, leading the way. "There are aliens everywhere."

"What kind?" asked Caine.

"The loathsome, dangerous, deadly kind," snapped Tootsie. "What other kind is there?"

"By 'what kind' I meant that I was referring to the stage of their life cycle," pontificated the android.

"Why? You want more samples?"

"No," demurred Caine. "I just want to know if I should be ready to brush them away from my face or hop out of their way."

"Mostly what we've got is the scuttling stage," said Tootsie, turning left down a dark, twisting corridor with a parked forklift with sinister shadows. "But some of the bigger ones are humping around there too. Larry fried one of the Curly-sized ones up with his handy flamethrower. It made a real big mess."

"What's wit' Curly?" asked Bruiser, clubbing a

scuttler with Slasher's pommel. "I didn't much like him. But seeing he was our only chance maybe getting outta here, well, I kinda miss him."

"It's just too horrible to explain," explained Tootsie with a delicate shudder. "Wait and see. He's just through here, in what used to be the nuclear reactor room."

"Used to be?" asked Bill, but before Tootsie could answer they were inside, and his eyes and nose told him all he wanted to know.

The huge room was filled with hundreds of small aliens that scuttled around in the cavern like fantastically ugly bees in an alien hive. But by far the most horrible thing was that Bill now knew what had happened to the rest of the crew from the communication station.

They hung on the wall like sides of beef, partially encased in weblike cocoons. They were mummies now, their life force long since sucked dry.

"Curly's over this way," said Tootsie and they dodged and stomped scuttlers to the far side of the room where Larry and Moe were keeping the aliens away from a fresh cocoon.

"He's moving," said Bill.

"They've been munching on him," said Moe. "Look at his ear." For once Bill could tell the clones apart; Larry had the flamethrower, Moe didn't, and Curly was the almost-mummy.

"But he's still got most of his life force," said Bruiser, bashing two scuttlers with a single blow from Slasher. "I t'ink he's trying to talk."

"It's hard to understand him with all that webbing covering his mouth," said Caine. "I believe he's either saying SAVE ME or KILL ME or FOR BOWB'S

SAKE DO SOMETHING. At least that's what it sounds like to me."

"Not to me," said Bill. "It sounds more like HELP! Let's get him out."

"Maybe not," said Bruiser. "If he wants us to kill him, maybe we should. I'm good at dat!"

"You been sniffing spores, Bruiser?" asked Rambette. "We can't kill the only one of us who knows how to fix the autopilot."

"Ahh, I forgot," said Bruiser sheepishly. "It's just dat I like to use Slasher."

"Well then, use Slasher to help me cut him loose," said Rambette, hacking and slicing at the cocoon.

While the two were up to their elbows in bits of cocoon, Bill's elephant foot embarked on a reflexive stomping spree, carrying him all around the room.

"If this weren't so life-threateningly dangerous, I'd find it most fascinating," said Caine, clubbing an alien with his flashlight. "This seems to be their primary feeding place."

"It seems to be a place I would like to get out of," said Bill, hopping away. "How's it going, Rambette?"

"We got Curly," she called. "Head for the door!"

"I'm heading where my foot takes me," cried Bill, stomping another scuttler and setting off towards a group of aliens crawling over the control board. "I may be here for years."

There were aliens everywhere, sadistically scuttling and nauseatingly nipping. For some unfathomable reason only the dog seemed untouched. The despicable creatures gave Barfer a wide berth.

"We gotta get outta here," shouted Bruiser, following Bill around the room, happily putting Slasher to good use. "Stop runnin' away!"

"I'm not—my foot is!" cried Bill, frantically following his foot to another cluster of scuttlers, losing his balance and falling into the crackling cocoon debris.

"Help me!" implored Tootsie. "My right arm's stuck in this cocoon!"

"Both of my right arms are stuck," shouted Bill.

Bruiser pulled Tootsie and Bill from their crunchy captivity and hefted Bill onto his shoulder. Bill's foot continued to try to stomp aliens, but since it couldn't reach the ground all it did was pound Bruiser on the back.

"Close the door!" cried Rambette as they tumbled out of the infested room. "Lock it!"

"What good is that going to do?" inquired Caine "We are dealing with incredibly powerful creatures."

"Shut your defeatist android yob," suggested Tootsie, pulling adhesive fragments off her right arm. "These creatures are worse than Chingers. We're all going to die!"

"There's a forklift parked down the corridor," said Caine. "Does anyone know how to work it?"

"Me," said Bill. "It's just like the one I drove back on the supply station."

"Then grab it and pile everything in sight that's heavy and bulky in front of the door," suggested Rambette. "Maybe that'll keep them in."

Bill started the forklift and in a few minutes had managed to build a remarkably tall stack of heavy junk in front of the door. They only saw two aliens during the operation, both of which were quickly dispatched by Slasher before Bill's foot had time to spring into action and drag him off the forklift.

"That ought to do it," said Rambette. "Let's head

back to the ship. Don't forget to bring all the repair supplies. I'm not coming back here for anything."

In their absence Uhuru had fashioned a new door to the docking tube, welding together chunks of heavy scrap metal. He was reluctant to open it until they convinced him that they were not harboring any aliens.

"I'm covering you with my flamethrower when you come in," he said, opening the door a crack. "Anything that scuttles gets fried."

"Nice flamethrower," said Larry as they filed into the ship. "It's lighter than mine."

"I made it out of the toaster," he said. "In times like these we must improvise. How's Curly?"

"A little chewed on, mostly in the ear department, but basically he's okay," said Moe. "At least as okay as he ever was which, P.S., is not saying very much."

"Someone has got to guard this door at all times," said Uhuru, still wearing his spacesuit. "We've got to keep the monsters at bay."

"I'll take first watch," said Larry. "While you get Curly patched up."

Upon examination in the control room, Curly's physical injuries turned out to be relatively minor, mainly consisting of a nibbled-on ear and a lot of ankle bites. His psychological condition, however, left a lot to be desired.

"You know how when something real bad happens you never remember it?" he asked as Caine wound a bandage around the victim's head.

"Sure," said Rambette. "It happens all the time. In total war you must expect anything. But, war may be hell but we must go through hell to defeat the evil of the Chingers..."

"Belt up!" Bill hinted. "You sound like a recruiting sergeant."

"I was! How bright of you to notice."

"I don't remember what happens to me after two beers," bragged Bruiser. "But I usually wake up in jail."

"It's a protective mechanism that helps people deal with traumatic events," explained Caine, tying the bandage with a fancy bow. "The mind trickily blocks threatening memories out as a form of protection."

"Well, my mind didn't block a single thing out this time," said Curly slowly. "I remember every horrible detail of that appalling experience. An alien nightmare! All those gnashing teeth! Those claws! That terrifying darkness filled with repulsive presences."

"You'll still be able to fix the autopilot, won't you?" asked Tootsie anxiously.

"Maybe," he muttered. "As long as I don't have alien flashback. I get the creeping horribles when I remember what happened."

"Stay calm," suggested Bill. "You're safe now. At least I think you are."

"That's a big help," said Tootsie, attending to the nips on her ankles. "We should all project positive attitudes."

"Look who's talking about attitude," said Rambette, taking off her boot and examining her wounded foot. "You ought to take yours back to the factory. Always moaning about how we're all going to die."

"It's probably true," moaned Tootsie.

"We're banged up, but still alive," said Bruiser. "I got lotsa bites myself, but got in plenty licks too, you betcha!"

"We all got wounded but Barfer," said Bill as the

dog walked in from the okra room munching on some buds.

"Maybe they don't like dogs," said Blight.

"If they like androids, they'll like dogs," said Caine. "It must be something else."

They all stared at Barfer, but he looked just as ugly and offensive as he always did.

"We gotta have more weapons," said Bruiser. "Heavy artillery, t'ings like dat."

"I'll make a flamethrower out of the microwave," said Moe. "Burn the bastards up!"

"You leave my microwave alone," snapped Uhuru. "That's reserved for food."

"Would you rather I made one out of the officers' urinals?" Moe eagerly asked. "I can build a flamethrower out of almost anything."

"How about bombs?" asked Bruiser. "Flamethrowers are okay, but bombs is great. Boom! Flying guts, gouts of fur, bits of alien!"

"I was thinking about something with a little more pinpoint accuracy," Rambette said. "Uhuru, can you make us some sort of hand grenades?"

"I need explosives for that," he said. "Lots of explosives."

"So make some," said Rambette. "I seem to recall you've done that before."

"Gunpowder," said Uhuru. "A primitive explosive from the dawn of time. I heard about it on a program once. It takes sulfur and charcoal."

"How *interesting*—we've got that in the potting room," said Caine. "Just don't take it all. I need the sulfur to adjust the pH of the okra's soil. It won't do to have the wrong pH. The okra might turn out even more bitter than it already is."

"But then I'll need potassium nitrate," said Uhuru. "Where will I get that?"

"In the kitchen," suggested Bill. "I know because I was going to be a Technical Fertilizer Operator. . . ."

"It's right next to the sugar, I suppose," Uhuru interrupted sarcastically.

"It's the same as saltpeter," said Bill. "Every trooper knows that the food is laced with saltpeter. It's supposed to keep our sex drive down. Even though it doesn't work too well."

"Is that true?" Moe asked Captain Blight.

"Well, it's just a *little* additive for the enlisted men," explained the captain. "Don't want them too raunchy on long trips."

"If you want some magnesium to spice up the mix, pull apart some flares," said Caine. "You will have an exceedingly explosive mixture."

"Sounds like a winner. I'll get on that," said Uhuru. "But we'll have to divide up the work. There's a lot to do. Who got the spare fuses?"

"I did," said Rambette.

"Okay, Bill starts on the fuses. The main bank's all blown and the circuit to the kitchen is giving us trouble each time I turn on the oven."

"Bill can drive a forklift, too," said Tootsie. "You should have seen him moving all that heavy junk."

"Good," said Uhuru. "We can use you for that, Bill. We need to move some steel plates out of the repair docks. It's a lucky thing we're on a repair ship. There are lots of vital parts here."

"I'd prefer to be on a killer-grade destroyer," said Bill. "That way we'd have what we need in the way of weapons."

"We've got to make do with what's at hand," said Uhuru. "No sense lamenting over what we don't have. Now, who brought back the silver screens?"

"Larry did," said Moe.

"No he didn't," said Tootsie. "He got the computer boards. I was with him the whole time. It wasn't on his list."

"Well, it was on somebody's list," said Uhuru. "Which dirty bowb forgot them? We need them to repair the shields. We can't lift off unless the shields are working."

Bill looked at his list. There it was: TWO ANODIZED SILVER SCREENS (2).

"I was busy," explained Bill. "I guess I forgot."

"We were all busy," snarled Rambette. "And the rest of us managed to get our shopping done while we were dodging aliens."

"You'll have to go back, Bill," said Uhuru grimly. "We need those screens."

CHAPTER 14

BILL WORKED HARD WITH THE FUSES SO he didn't even have to think about the screen problem. It was comforting, specialized work that he had trained hard to master. Put fuse in, take fuse out. The most skilled part was reading the little numbers stamped on the end of each fuse. The numbers were always faint and nearly impossible to make out. Bill was proud of his technical skill. Actually, he kind of liked fuses. They either worked or they didn't. Fuses had very little middle ground, and they didn't waffle around much. Besides, these were small fuses, not like the huge ones he'd had to manhandle in the battleships. As an added benefit, fuses were almost always located away from the places most people went, so he had some time to himself.

He was enjoying the quiet, moronic work, testing an entire bank of fuses, when Rambette came into the fuse chamber and started talking to him.

"I've got wire splicing detail," she said, brandishing one of her sharpest knives and cutting the insulation off a strand of orange cable. "This ship is pretty banged up."

"Tell me about it. It's a good thing for all of you that I'm a skilled fusetender," he said humbly. "I think I've got enough blown fuses to fill the station's basement."

Rambette shuddered delicately. "Don't mention that place to me—I still got nightmares."

"It seems like there's a creeping horror behind every door these days," mused Bill, zapping a fuse with a sizzling load of volts. "Bruiser killed two in the galley. Blight composted them. Makes great fertilizer he says. What do you hear about Curly?"

"Except for his ear, he seems all right. He's busy digging into the autopilot now. He should be okay. But I think I sprained my andromeda back there."

"I never heard of one of those," Bill said.

"A lot you know! *I* know an andromeda strain when I get one," snapped Rambette. "They're pure agony. Here, hold this orange wire."

"Sure," said Bill, taking it in one of his right hands.

"Now grab this yellow one," said Rambette, handing him another wire which he took in his other right hand.

"Yow!" shrieked Bill, getting a jolt of juice that made his hair curl and his tusks smoke.

"Good," said Rambette. "They're both live. That's what I needed to know. Hold them while I splice them together."

"Yow!" cried Bill. "Yow!"

"That's great," said Rambette, wrapping tape around the wires. "I'm all through now. See you later."

"Yow!" Bill yowed one last time.

It took about five minutes for his hands to stop tingling enough to let him grab and pull the next fuse. It checked out a dud, and he was trying to read the number when Caine came in.

"Oh, there you are, Bill," he said. "I've been looking for you."

"You found me," he grumped. "Now get lost. I have work to do."

"I want to run a theory by you," said the android. "Send it up the flagpole, so to speak, and see who salutes it. Listen. Since we got back on the ship and are relatively safe for the moment, my scientific curiosity has returned with increased vigor."

"You're not planning some dumb thing like smuggling some deadly aliens back in a jar, are you?" Bill asked with suspicious horror.

"I'm not *that* curious. But I'll no doubt get a delightful research paper out of this horrible experience. I'll be famous, and if you aid me you will be cited as reference material. Assuming, of course, that we get out of this difficult situation alive."

"Would you kindly keep that kind of bowb to yourself and get out of here."

"No, listen, I'm serious. I have the life cycles of the creatures almost completely worked out. When we arrived they somehow sensed an increase in the available food supply—they are undoubtedly sensitive to the essence of life, the *élan vital* that flows through all living creatures—and hatched out a new generation. The older ones that were around when we arrived must have been feeding off what remained of the mummified crew. Isn't that a wonderful scenario?"

"Delightful," sneered Bill, who did not care to be considered snack food for aliens.

"I knew you would see the beauty in such a complex and monstrously malevolent life form," said Caine happily. "The others refuse to listen to me."

"With very good reason, you sadistic android!" Bill shouted. "Now get out!"

Caine, carried away by his theories, ignored the suggestion. Eyes gleaming with inspiration, finger raised lecturingly, he went on. "I postulate that each step in the life cycle is larger and more dangerous than the previous stage. So far the biggest ones we've seen are the Curly-sized variety, but that is surely not their upper limit. If you're lucky, you might see an even larger one when you return to get the screens."

"Would you kindly shut your gob," groaned Bill.

"Even if you do, I don't suppose you'll be able to collect a sample for me," Caine hinted smarmily, then dodged when Bill reached for him. "Of course, I understand, that's really too much to ask. But I could use a really detailed description. Measurements would help, too. Be sure to be objective when you run up against one. Take your time, make notes. I can't have any muddled reports in my paper."

"I'm going to kill you if you don't leave now," said Bill, looking for a really heavy fuse to bash the bowb's head in with.

"You can't mean that, Bill. Look on this as a service to science. And if you're real, *real* lucky, you might even meet up with the queen."

"Royalty here?" asked Bill.

"A technical and scientific term usually used to refer to an insect progenitor. Something must be laying all those eggs. She's probably huge, much larger than the Curly-sized ones. And dangerous, too. Nothing in nature is as violent as a mother protecting her young. I'd give a lot to be able to observe that."

"Done! You can go instead of me," Bill shouted happily.

"Thanks for the kind offer—but I need to survive to write my research paper, and whoever meets up with the mother is not likely to come back alive. To tell you the truth, I think I'll have to omit that part from my report. I'll have to be satisfied with conjecture about that stage of the life cycle. I'll keep it logical and consistent. I'm sure that a single slight omission shouldn't keep me from being published."

"That's good," lied Bill, lifting a fuse—not heavy enough to beat out the android's brains with. "What the universe really needs now is a scientific paper about alien monsters."

"See? I knew you'd understand. Well, I must be back to my repairs. The okra room is a mess. Talking with you has been a big help. See you later."

The fuse crashed into the door an instant after he closed it. Once again Bill lapsed into the grateful, depressed silence. A Trooper could gather his thoughts alone like this. To think things over, a good place to worry, a good place to get scared to death at every little noise.

Suddenly it didn't seem as quiet as it had been. There were lots of little creaks and groans that Bill sincerely hoped were just the sounds of metal snapping with temperature changes. There were faint rustling and scuttling noises that Bill earnestly prayed were simply rodents.

Scuttle? Bill looked fearfully around, but there was nothing out of the ordinary in sight. His elephant foot twitched ominously. Hadn't Rambette said they killed two of the aliens within the ship? If two, why not three? Four? A hundred? Bill shuddered and quickly shoved a fuse into place. He was sweating now, his hands shaking. His moment of peace was ended. He had to finish quickly and get back to the others. Being alone with hidden, crawling, deadly creatures that could be lurking in every shadow was a form of suicide. The scuttling and scratching grew louder. Bill dropped a fuse. Something moved!

"Yow!" screamed Bill, jumping back and raising his elephant foot high in the air. "Yow!"

"Don't stomp me, Bill," cried a seven-inch-high Chinger, waving all four arms in the air. "You'll only hurt your foot. Don't you remember me?"

"Eager Beager? Is that you?" asked Bill, stopping his foot in midstomp with the greatest of difficulty.

"None other," said the little green creature.

"How'd you get here?" Bill asked.

"Easily. Through the door down by that docking tube. It was open and the cretin on guard with the homemade flamethrower was taking a nap. I'd keep it closed if I was you. And hang the guard up by the thumbs. This is a dangerous place."

"But how'd you get here?" Bill asked in wonderment. "I mean to this planet, at this time?"

"The Chinger ship I was on heard your automatic distress signal when you crash-landed, and came to investigate. Though you are our enemies, by your own choosing of course, we are still moral creatures and we would help any survivors. But not this time. When we realized which planet this was we decided to keep our distance."

"Tootsie was right," moaned Bill. "We're going to die, killed by aliens one way or another. If the cocoon aliens don't get us, you little green ones will."

"Knock off the paranoia, Bill. Have I ever attempted to harm you? Your military indoctrination is showing. And, incidentally, I don't really consider myself an alien," said Eager Beager. "To me, you're the alien. But, philosophical questions aside, you really don't have much to worry about from us Chingers here."

"That's a relief," said Bill. "It may have taken you thousands of years to discover fighting, but you picked it up quick."

"Only in self-defense, to save what we hold near and dear. And we're not hanging around here very long. It's far too dangerous. We've known about this planet for years and make great efforts to avoid the place. It amused us greatly when you decided to build a communications station here. It was a masterstroke of sheer stupidity."

"That's the military mind for you," agreed Bill. "If it's stupid or criminal don't look for an intelligent way out—just send in the troops."

"But the truly incredible part is how you managed to build the station right on top of the alien's nest. That's like standing on the only anthill in the middle of a desert. Even the dumbest bowb would move a couple steps to one side. Proving once again that 'military intelligence' is formed by two mutually incompatible words."

"But it wasn't *my* fault the ship came here. We had little choice. And besides, someone else made the decisions."

"Now *that* is a train of logic that's dangerous and murky as all get-out," said Eager Beager. "I think that falls into the domain of 'I was just following orders.' A lot of evil has been perpetrated in the universe by people abandoning intelligence and thinking that way. Abrogating your responsibility by blaming it on others might be temporarily good for your mental health, but somewhere along the line somebody has to answer for everything."

"Sure," Bill agreed, having lost track of the complex argument, his brain cells deadened by years of military discipline. He changed the subject before he could be forced to think. "By the way, you wouldn't happen to know how's the war going? I've been out of touch on this ship."

"It's going quite well, or badly, depending on your perspective."

"Who's winning?" asked Bill.

"No one's winning, airhead!" shouted the Chinger. "Or, rather, each side is claiming to be winning, which is exactly the same thing. There are battles being fought in almost every corner of the galaxy. The body counts, even adjusting for inflation, are staggering."

"The Emperor is quite fond of this war," sighed Bill. "He'll keep it up as long as he can. It's good for the economy and keeps a lot of people employed, mostly us Troopers."

"But we both know it's senseless and can't be won by either side. It's not logical to continue."

"Logic has never been the strong point of the military mind," said Bill. "But how did you figure out *I* was here?"

"We were listening in on your radio communications when I discovered you were on the ship," said the Chinger, leaning back and resting on his little tail. "I thought I'd drop in and see how your pacification efforts were coming along."

"Well," evaded Bill. "I've had my hands full lately."

"It can't be more important than ending this senseless war," said Eager Beager. "Nothing's more important than that."

"I've had day-to-day survival on my mind," said Bill. "Stomping aliens and trying to stay one step ahead of the grim reaper has been keeping me pretty busy."

"As I recall you agreed to sow dissension and spread propaganda for us," said the Chinger. "That was the deal for your new foot. And, speaking of your foot, what happened to it? That thing you've got on the end of your leg is the ugliest excuse for a foot I've ever seen. It looks like it belongs on a large, gray mammal."

"It's a long story," said Bill. "I traded your old one in, and this is what I got stuck with."

"I could probably arrange to get you a new foot in exchange for vital information and war secrets. They don't mean anything, but we are beginning to develop a military class that is just as stupid as your military class. That is the *real* horror of this war."

"Actually, this foot has turned out to be kind of useful," said Bill, tapping it up and down. "In our current desperate situation it's handy to have a stomping device with you at all times."

"Suit yourself. But I would really like to see more constructive peaceful effort on your part. I am putting myself to considerable risk making contact with you, and it seems the least you could do in return is bend a few minds in the right direction."

"I did take part in a mutiny."

"That's a good step," said the Chinger. "The erosion of authority can lead to independent thought. Once the teeming masses start questioning the actions of those who seek power, maybe we can break the chains of stupidity that keep us locked in this idiotic conflict."

"Oh," said Bill. "I guess I can give you the ship's destination and cargo. That's probably a secret or something."

"It's probably a worthless secret," said the Chinger, "because in all likelihood you'll never survive long enough to leave this planet. Lay it on me anyway."

"We're bound for Beta Draconis," said Bill. "And we've got a load of okra."

"I knew it would be worthless information," said Eager Beager. "There's nothing in Beta Draconis but a bunch of busted ships. We really whipped you there. If I didn't hate this war so badly, I'd be real proud of our side. And what's with the okra? Taste treats for the overworked troops?"

"It's more like a hobby the captain has," said Bill. "He grows it, but he doesn't eat it."

"I'll never understand you humans," said the Chinger, throwing three of his arms in the air and scratching his tummy with the fourth. "Always engaged in senseless activities."

"It's not exactly senseless. My dog likes the okra."

"That's what I mean," said Eager Beager. "Did you know humans are the only creatures in the universe that keep other creatures as pets? Kind of makes you wonder, doesn't it."

"I never gave it much thought," admitted Bill.

"I detect someone coming down the hall," said the Chinger. "I've got to get going. I don't know if I'll get back here or not, since our crew is anxious to exit this menacing planet. I want you to know that even if you die and are no use to me anymore, you've been a pretty nice human, as humans go."

"Thanks, I think," said Bill. "The feeling is mutual, little feller."

"If you survive this, don't forget to keep on sowing dissension," said Eager Beager, tearing an opening in the metal wall and scuttling through it. "If you don't survive, forget it."

"What was that?" asked Uhuru, coming into the utility room. "Did I see something scuttle away just now? Were you talking to someone?"

"It was nothing," lied Bill. "I was reading the numbers off the fuses to myself."

"It's hard to see anything through this fogged-up faceplate," said Uhuru, smearing it with a gloved hand. "And these rotten little lights cause a lot of glare. I wish I could turn them off. I don't need them except in the dark anyway."

"I'm just about finished with the fuses," said Bill.

"Forget the fuses," said Uhuru. "We need those screens right away. It's time for you to go back to that cavern of certain doom."

CHAPTER 15

"TAKE THIS FLAMETHROWER," SAID MOE as they were outfitting Bill in the control room. "I made it myself out of a sump pump."

"And here are some grenades," said Uhuru. "They're kind of delicate. Try not to bump into anything. You can hang them from your belt."

"Take one of my knives," offered Rambette. "Not that one, it's my best, my favorite. I won't tell you about the throats . . . Take one of the others. It's just that since you probably won't be coming back alive, I don't want to lose my best knife, too. You understand."

"Yeah, yeah," Bill muttered in numb incomprehension. He was beyond understanding anything, now that fear had occupied almost all of his brain.

"Don't forget my observations," Caine reminded him. "I want a clear and concise report when you run across the aliens."

"Just where am I going?" Bill complained, at the

same time making an obscene gesture in the direction of the asinine android. "Does anyone know where I'm supposed to find these screens?"

"They're probably stored in the supply dock," said Captain Blight. "You can't miss the place, it's right next to the reactor room that's filled with all those repulsive aliens."

"Wonderful," muttered Bill. "And what do these screens look like?"

"They're anodized aluminum," said Uhuru. "About twenty feet tall and fifty feet wide. They'll probably be rolled up."

"Wait a minute!" snapped Bill. "How can I carry something like that?"

"Under your arm," suggested Uhuru. "They're extremely thin and not very heavy."

"They might not be heavy, but they're long," said Bill. "Even if they've been rolled lengthwise, they're still twenty feet long. I'd have to drag them and I'd bash them about while I was dodging and killing aliens. Do you want scraped and bent screens?"

"Don't even think of that!" cried Uhuru. "The screens are precision-milled to very tight tolerances. I guess we'll have to send somebody else along to help you. Any volunteers?"

"Count me out," moaned Tootsie, who was the only one to respond in any way to the call for volunteers. Other than a quick shuffle as they all moved back.

"Let's not all speak at once," said Uhuru. "Maybe we should draw straws."

"I'm wise to you and your straws," said Rambette. "Put them away."

"Okay," said Uhuru. "We can use this other set I've got here." He shook the cut lengths of tubing out onto the table, pointed out that one was shorter than the others, then took them in one hand and shuffled them so that the short end could not be seen.

"That sounds fair to me," Tootsie said reluctantly, choosing a straw.

"Life was sure a lot easier when all I had to do was order some poor bowb to do the crappy jobs," complained Captain Blight, closing his eyes and taking a straw. "Doing things in a democratic fashion is not a process that I really enjoy."

"I got da short one," cried Bruiser happily. "It's you and me, Bill! And da odds ain't good. I hope you ready to die like a man?"

"Not really," admitted Bill.

"Ohh, it's a Trooper's lot," intoned Uhuru. "One is either bored out of one's skull, or frightened out of one's pants. Indeed, I do wish that I could go with you, but I've got to get the shields ready for the screens, just in case you manage to come back alive."

"Thanks much," Bill sneered, instantly recognizing self-serving cowardice.

"Gotta get a flamethrower, Moe," said Bruiser. "I ain't going down dere without one."

"I made this one out of a refrigeration coil," said Moe proudly. "Be careful, it's loaded with high-test rocket fuel."

"Give me your good knife, Rambette," said Bruiser. "It might come in handy."

"No way," snapped Rambette.

"If they don't come back, it's not going to do you any good, is it?" said Tootsie with impeccable logic. "Hand it over."

"You don't know what you're asking," Rambette cried. "My mother gave me it at the coming-of-age ceremony, when I got my first bat. It's all I've got left from her, the only memory of that fair world so distant. It would be like you giving away Slasher."

"I never do dat," said Bruiser. "But we need dat knife. Give—or I take it."

"Why are we fighting among ourselves?" moaned Tootsie. "Don't we have enough of an enemy out there without turning on each other?"

"It's nerves," said Caine. "A typical human reaction to overwhelming fear is to strike out at whatever—or whoever—is nearest."

"Are you calling me a coward, you hunk of tin?" shouted Rambette. "You men are all alike, even you android men. Think a woman can't take it? I'll show you! Give me your flamethrower, Uhuru, I'm going in. If we depend on these two clumsy bowbs to bring the screens back we might as well throw in the towel."

"Show these mothers what real women can do!" cheered Tootsie. "Whoopee!"

"I'm keeping my flamethrower," said Uhuru, clutching it to him.

"Take this one," said Moe. "I fabricated it out of some spare radio parts and an enema bag."

"Why are you two bowbs standing there with your mouths hanging open?" Rambette snapped, grabbing the makeshift flamethrower from Moe. "Let's move out!"

"We go!" howled Bruiser, waving Slasher whistling in the air. "It's time to kill, destroy—good stuff!"

Bill reluctantly followed Bruiser and Rambette to the docking tube, where their hooting and hollering—and a few well-aimed kicks—woke up the dormant Larry. Bill was glad to see that Eager Beager had closed the door behind him when he left.

"I'm going in first," snapped Rambette, kicking the door open and spraying the tube with a billowing blast of flame. "You two follow me. Keep low and don't shoot until we get out of the tube. I'm not getting fried by one of you trigger-happy bowbs."

Bill was only too glad to follow those kind of instructions, and ducked into the smoking tube in front of Bruiser. The middle seemed like the safest place. It wasn't, he rationalized as they snaked down the dark tube, that he was a coward. It was simply an applied strategy that took survival factors into account and weighed them very heavily. And covered his ass.

"Get ready," said Rambette as they neared the entrance to the station. "Everyone come out firing. On the count of three. One! Two! *Go for it!*"

Bill was a little slow because he was waiting for three, being a literal-minded, order-following Trooper. But when Bruiser ran over him and knocked him out of the tube into the anteroom, he triggered the flamethrower and blasted everything in sight.

"I got 'em!" he cried. "Look at 'em burn!"

"You fried the spacesuits," said Rambette dourly. "There're no aliens here."

"Maybe they were hiding in the spacesuits," said Bill, scrambling for an excuse. "That's it, they were probably just waiting for us to walk by and then they'd jump out and get us. We wouldn't have had a chance."

"Right," said Rambette. "I'll believe that the day you pass an IQ test."

"Troopers don't take IQ tests, just officers," Bill explained.

"Dere's a baked alien in dis spacesuit," called

Bruiser, inspecting the smoldering mess. "And another one in here."

Rambette looked at Bill with newfound admiration. "You know how to call them," she said admiringly. "Sorry about the IQ thing. Maybe you ought to take point and lead us in."

"You're doing fine," said Bill quickly. "Keep up the good work."

"Let's do it then! Through this door, down the corridor. Let's clear the way first."

Bruiser kicked the door open, and Rambette tossed one of Uhuru's grenades in and jumped back. A tremendous explosion rocked the corridor, and smoke came boiling back into the anteroom.

"I just love dat noise," said Bruiser happily. "Can I throw one too?"

"Save them," said Rambette as the smoke settled. "We'll need them later. Follow me!"

Bill stuck as closely as possible to Rambette, holding his flamethrower tightly with both right arms. Bruiser was treading on his heels as they moved in cautious hurry down the door-lined corridor.

"Move!" cried Bruiser, shoving Bill in the back. An instant later the first room off the corridor erupted with a roar.

"I maybe saw something move," said Bruiser. "Uhuru makes good grenade."

"Quit playing games," snapped Rambette. "We've got to get the screens."

Two seconds later, the second and third rooms off the corridor blasted into oblivion. Bruiser was smiling guiltily and Rambette called a halt.

"Is there something moving in every room?" she asked sarcastically. "If you keep blasting away we're not going to have any grenades left when we really need them."

"Hard to stop," grinned Bruiser. "Great fun. Boom, boom!"

"Knock it off!" Bill ordered, remembering that he was the MP in charge. "Save the grenades for when we need them."

"I'll try," muttered Bruiser. "Hard to do. Bruiser is super Trooper, bad-to-the-bone killing machine. Don't like sit around. Get fidgety and want to be chopping someone's legs off. Kill, maim—dat's my way."

"All we're asking you to do is go a little easy," said Rambette, leading them up to the reactor room. "At least wait until you see the greens of their eyes."

"Maybe he shouldn't wait quite that long," suggested Bill. "I'm all for taking them out at first sight."

"He's right!" Bruiser enthused. "You talking real Trooper talk."

"Wow!" said Rambette. "Look at that!"

The door to the reactor room was holding, but just barely. Great gashes had been cut through it from the inside, and molten metal dripped from the fresh cuts like metallic lava.

"They must have some pretty strong acid," said Bill. "I'm glad Caine isn't here. He'd probably want us to collect samples."

"The supply dock is down here," called Rambette. "Behind this door."

"Oh boy," said Bruiser. "Can I throw da grenade in dis time? Please?"

"No grenades, bowb-brain," sneered Rambette. "You want to blow those screens full of holes? Uhuru said to be careful with them."

"Maybe little flamethrower burn-burn?" asked Bruiser hopefully.

"Forget it," ordered Rambette.

"Maybe we should just open the door and look inside," suggested Bill. "It's more than possible that we've already lost any element of surprise with all that grenade banging."

"Bruiser no do t'ings half way." The burly moron raised Slasher over his head. "Do it—no talk about it!"

Before they could stop him, Bruiser knocked the door from its hinges with a single blow from his axe. It dropped to the floor with a loud clang.

"That was real subtle," said Bill, backing away from the door. "They'll never guess we're out here."

"I don't see any aliens inside," said Rambette, standing in the open doorway with her flamethrower ready.

"That's a big place," said Bill, coming up to stand beside her. "You could hide a hundred aliens in there."

The supply dock was immense, large enough to hold a ship the size of the *Bounty* and have enough room to spare for a squadron of fighters. Packing crates and moving equipment were scattered all around the metal-grate floor. Stacks of steel beams, easily a hundred feet long, were dwarfed to matchstick size by the gargantuan proportions of the mammoth structure; the nearby forklift looked like a toy.

"I don't see the screens," said Bill.

"They could be anywhere," said Rambette, inching her way carefully into the supply dock. "We'll have to go in and look for them. Come on. Keep your eyes open for movement."

Her last warning, as far as Bill was concerned, was

totally unnecessary. His finger twitched and tightened on the flamethrower's trigger as he followed Rambette. His nerves, already honed to a fine edge by the overwhelming danger, passed into the outer limits of stuttering panic. If he saw so much as a roach, he'd roast it.

"There!" cried Rambette, dropping to her knees and raising her flamethrower. "Over there. Move, Bruiser! I can't get a clean shot!"

A larger-than-Curly-sized alien rose out from behind a stack of boxes by Bruiser. It hissed and snarled, dripping ichor and clashing its pointed teeth. One clawed hand swung out and wrestled Slasher away from Bruiser, throwing the axe a hundred yards with the ease of a Trooper throwing back a beer. Then, with an angry swish of its ridged tail, it leaped out and grabbed the big man.

"Dis t'ing's choking me!" choked out Bruiser. "It's got my ear! My throat! Aggg!"

Rambette drew her mother's knife and leaped toward the alien. For an instant she stood frozen, poised in front of the huge beast, crouched low and ready to spring. The alien held the struggling Bruiser easily and looked down on the woman as if she were an insignificant insect.

"Take this, you bowing acned alien!" she cried, jumping up and slashing at the creature. "The Emperor forever! Death to all grundgies! Die!"

Surprised by the fierce attack, the alien dropped Bruiser to the ground and grabbed Rambette, twisting her in the air like a doll. Then it threw her on top of Bruiser and loomed over them, drooling ichor and dripping gore.

Bill seized the moment and ran forward, sticking his flamethrower into the heaving ribs of the monstrous creature. Before it could react he pulled the trigger, flames washing out. The results were impressive. The creature burst into flame and exploded into a giant cloud of smoke.

"They must dry out when they get big," Bill said. "We better remember that."

"Nice style, Bill," said Rambette, wiping ichor off her knife. "I couldn't have done better myself."

Bruiser climbed to his feet and looked around, scowling. "Where's my Slasher?"

"Somewhere over thataway," said Bill.

"Got to get Slasher. Be back quick."

"Look for the screens over there, too," called Rambette, checking her flamethrower. "I've had enough of this place. I wish I was anyplace else but here, like in some bar, sipping Galactic Garglers with a good friend. Drunk with one drink—stone dead with two."

"Sounds great," Bill lied as they started combing through the stacked supplies. They found about a thousand cases marked dehydrated toilet paper, but no screens.

"Whoa!" called Bruiser. "Look at dat!"

"Did you find the screens?" asked Bill as he and Rambette hurried across to the spot where Bruiser was on his knees looking down into something.

"Not here. Found Slasher," said Bruiser. "And dis."

It was a huge hole in the metal floor, its edges eaten away by what could only have been alien acid. An enormous orange-fur-littered tunnel led from the opening into the darkness below.

"I don't think the screens are down there," said

Rambette. "It looks like it might go all the way back down to the pod cavern."

"I'm not going to be the one to check it out," said Bruiser. "*Hey!* What's dat?"

"Something's moving down there," cried Rambette. "Something impossibly large and covered with orange fur and ichor."

"I think we're going to meet mother," moaned Bill. "And I don't think she'll be happy that we've been killing her kids."

CHAPTER **16**

THE MONSTROUS MOTHER MONSTER, menacingly malignant, rose slowly out of the hole. With terrible certainty, a gigantic clawed hand, twice as large as Bruiser, gripped the edge of the floor. Then a second hand appeared, and a third, followed by her immense sloping head, its multiple rows of pointed teeth clashing and gnashing as she drooled noxious ichor and breathed in and out with a terrible reverberating rasping sound that, like one coffin being dragged across another, sent a cold chill up Bill's back.

He started backing away as the creature continued to pull itself out onto the supply dock. The mother towered high over the three Troopers, grunting and hissing as it freed first one enormous leg and then the other. And the other. And two more. Its huge tail swung out and barely missed pounding Bruiser into an unrecognizable splotch.

"Run!" suggested Bill.

"Toss da grenades!" shouted Bruiser.

"Take the mother out!" cried Rambette.

"This way!" yelled Bill, who had already opted for running instead of fighting and was headed full-tilt toward the part of the supply dock that was the most crowded with boxes and crates. "If we hide, maybe she won't be able to find us."

"Clear thinking," cried Rambette. "Come on, Bruiser. Let's follow Bill."

"Can't I just—*Yeow!*—dat was too close. I t'ink maybe you right!"

The trio ducked behind a stack of packing crates each bearing the label TOILET PAPER, DEHYDRATED, 10,000 ROLLS, ADD WATER AND STEP BACK. Bill fervently hoped they hadn't been shipped by mistake instead of the screens. This kind of thing happened far too often.

The malevolent beast was tromping and crashing around the supply dock, roaring and dripping ichor. Its spiked tail swung in a wide and murderous arc, pulverizing anything it crashed into. The creature seemed to be moving randomly, pushing crates aside as though they weighed nothing at all. Then it paused, rotated its enormous head slowly, and stared right at the humans' hiding place.

"Gonna get it!" cried Bruiser, tossing two grenades. "Turn you into green hamburger!"

Bill hit the deck to avoid the fragments. The grenades exploded with a tumultuous roar. "Did we get her?" he asked, his face on the floor. "Did it tear her apart?"

"Not all," said Bruiser. "Nicked couple of places, dat's all. Maybe oozing bit more. If we had couple thousand grenades, do okay—*Wow!*—here dat t'ing comes!"

"I'll back her up with the flamethrower!" yelled Rambette. "Bruiser, cover me! Bill, get that forklift over there!"

"You want me to fight this alien with a forklift?" asked Bill. "You out of your teeny-tiny? You been into the spores again?"

"Do you see any battle-tanks around here?" sneered Rambette. "We've got to go with what we've got. Move, bowb-brain!"

Bill glanced over his shoulder as he ran for the forklift, his elephant foot leaving dents in the floor. The alien mother was awash with fire as both Bruiser and Rambette had their weapons on maximum strength. The creature was a towering inferno, but except for being bathed in flames, it seemed little the worse for wear. It wasn't combustible like the other giant aliens. But it was certainly angry, and roared at earsplitting volume while it thrashed around violently.

Bill leaped on the forklift, started it and put it in gear. The nearest thing even remotely resembling a weapon was a pile of steel girders, so he picked a few up and angled them out like spears.

"Get her, Bill," cried Bruiser. "Hurry! She's gaining on us."

Bill figured there was a slightly faint and very remote chance he might be able to force the creature back into the hole. If he did that, they could maybe close it up with the grenades. It wouldn't hold her long, but it might buy them enough time to find the screens and get out of this death trap. He headed toward the alien, shifting into high gear. It all sounded very iffy—but there was no other choice.

"Dat's it, Trooper," cried Bruiser as Bill crashed

into the mother monster with a Bill-bruising jolt. "I fry and you push."

"Over here," shouted Rambette. "I found the screens."

"Dat's it, Bill," said Bruiser, backing away. "You push—and I'll help Rambette with da screens."

Bill had serious reservations about this recent modification of his careful plan. He was not happy being a steel-girder length away from the killer creature without a lot of firepower backing him up.

The creature, still smoldering and screaming with pain, or bad temper, or both, weaved and dodged like a punch-drunk prizefighter. It slipped around to one side of the girders and almost had Bill by the throat when he spun the forklift hard and blindsided the beast, toppling her to her multiple knees. He slammed into reverse gear and backed off, preparing for another futile attack.

"We got 'em, Bill," shouted Rambette. "Come on!"

He didn't need to be told twice. Bill dropped the girders, hit the throttle with all the weight his elephant foot could manage and went screeching toward the door, crashing through the gear box and laying a smoking track of burning rubber behind him. As he got to the door, he slammed on the brakes, locked the wheels and slid sideways through the opening.

"Did you get your driver's license in a cereal box?" laughed Rambette, stacking grenades in the door opening. Bill and Bruiser frantically loaded the screens on the front of the forklift.

"Here she comes!" cried Rambette, jumping on the back of the forklift with Bruiser. "Hit it!"

Bill grabbed the first forward gear he could find and mashed the throttle again. The monstrous mother alien was almost on them. Rambette sprayed the pile of grenades with her flamethrower and the resulting explosion rocked the corridor and almost lifted the forklift into the air.

"Wow!" cried Bruiser as the dust and forklift settled to the ground. "Dat was close."

"Is the door blocked?" asked Bill, too busy motoring down the corridor to look back at the debris-clogged doorway.

"I hope so," said Rambette. "Can't you go any faster?"

"I'm doing the best—*Yow!*" Bill cranked the steering wheel hard and with twin bumps ran over two aliens. They were the scuttling kind, and his elephant foot started twitching enthusiastically.

"Look up there!" cried Rambette. "They've broken out of the reactor room."

The area was swarming with orange-furred repellent aliens of all sizes, from the cute little fur-and-feather babies to the Curly-sized stomping uglies. What used to have been the door to the reactor room was a pile of molten slag. Ichor and fur were everywhere as Bill went into a stomach-wrenching four-wheel slide.

"Don't hurt the screens!" cried Rambette, as Bill fought for control of the skidding forklift.

"Yippee!" yelled Bruiser, tossing a grenade into a flock of swarming aliens. "To da left, Rambette! Burn dem!"

A cluster of creatures went up in flames as Rambette sprayed them with liquid fire. It was all pretty revolting. Even as they melted, others scrambled to take their place.

Bruiser threw another grenade and shouted. "Look! Here come da reinforcements!"

"Ours or theirs?" cried Bill hopefully, fighting the wheel.

"Two guesses," Rambette panted gloomily.

The corridor was filled with gnashing and struggling aliens, clawing their way over each other to get to the fleeing forklift and its edible, spawnable passengers. Bruiser shifted to his flamethrower and sprayed them until it ran out of rocket fuel. He used it to club a few of the nearest creatures back and finally threw it in the face of a Curly-sized one.

"I taking yours," he cried, grabbing Bill's weapon and blasting a dozen aliens that were trying to climb aboard. "Da docking tube's over dere! Make it quick!"

Bill skidded around the corner and hit the brakes hard, screeching to a stop by the entrance to the docking tube. While he was unfastening his seat belt, Rambette and Bruiser jumped off.

"We've got all kinds of creeping horrors on the silver screens," cried Rambette. "They're nightmare material for sure!"

About a dozen of the scuttlers were scuttling around on the screens. Bill struggled and danced in circles trying to keep his elephant foot from stomping them, rendering the vitally important screens useless in the process.

"I've got dem!" cried Bruiser happily.

"No grenades!" howled Rambette. "And absolutely no flamethrowers!"

"Just use Slasher," Bruiser slavered happily, grinning and picking them off one by one, using his axe with a surgeon's precision.

"I got this end," said Bill, grabbing the screens. "Bruiser, you take the other. Rambette, cover our retreat."

"You got it, Trooper," said Rambette, spraying the anteroom with her flamethrower.

Bill lifted his end and led Bruiser up the tube. Rambette tossed a few good-luck grenades to make sure they weren't being followed, while Bruiser leaned out and sprayed the tube ahead with his flamethrower to clear the way. Larry opened the door when they arrived and slammed it tight behind them. The whole crew was gathered in hopeful anticipation.

"Bad out dere," said Bruiser, soot-faced and sweaty. "But we do wotta Trooper gotta do."

"Grammatically unsound but commendable," said Christianson. "But we have been suffering too, you know. The latrines are backed up again."

"The screens!" cried Uhuru. "About twenty minutes work and we can get out of here. Come on, Larry. Give me a hand."

"I got the autopilot working," said Curly as Larry and Uhuru hauled the screens away. "At least I think it's working. It probably is. Maybe. Maybe not."

"Ichor flashbacks," whispered Captain Blight. "Sometimes he gets confused."

"It should be okay," said Curly. "It'll take us straight to Beta Draconis. Or maybe it'll drop us into a dark star somewhere. But, gee, all a guy can do is try."

"I'm most interested in the alien situation," said Caine. "What did you discover?"

"You were right about the mother," gasped Bill, slumping exhaustedly to the floor. "We met her."

"Wonderful!" cried Caine. "And you lived to tell me about it. This is fantastic news. My report will be acclaimed on every inhabited planet. I'm back to my future as a renowned scientist. What did she look like?"

"Real big," said Bruiser.

"Could you possibly quantify that in some detail?" asked Caine. "Real big is hardly scientific. How big is big? Did anyone take measurements?"

"Ugly, too," said Rambette. "Ugliest alien I've ever seen."

"Could you possibly define that with just a little more objectivity?" moaned Caine. "I don't believe I can use the word *ugly* in my paper."

"Dangerous," said Bill. "A hard-shelled, multi-legged horror dripping ichor and orange fur all over the place."

"Did you kill it?" asked Curly anxiously. "Or will I have to worry about it and maybe mess up the autopilot?"

"It didn't look too good the last time I saw it," said Bill, stretching the truth elastically.

"I really must have more concrete details for my report," said Caine. "Didn't *anybody* take measurements?"

"Will you bowb off," suggested Bill. "We'll catch you up later. If we want to. Let's get the ship out of here first."

"There is one small problem," said Tootsie hesitantly. "It's your dog, Barfer."

"Hey," said Bill. "Where is he? I don't know why, but for some reason I miss the smelly brute."

"Well, he missed you too," said Tootsie. "He really whined and fussed when you went out after the screens."

"That's my good dog for you," said Bill. "He knows how much I like him."

"He's gone," moaned Tootsie. "Gone."

"What?" shrieked Bill. "Is he in the okra room?"

"He's in the communication station, Bill," said

Curly. "He got by Larry just after you left, and went down the docking tube. He's out there all alone with all those horrible ichor zombies. Yow!"

"The poor dog's helpless," moaned Tootsie. "You can't seriously be thinking of leaving him behind."

"I'm thinking," said Bill. "Don't rush me. I'm thinking."

"He depends on you," said Captain Blight. "Only the lowest form of life would turn his back on a friend."

"That dog loves you," said Rambette. "What are you going to do?"

"Fifteen minutes to liftoff," said Uhuru through the intercom. "If anybody's got anything else to do, they better do it quickly."

Bill sighed emphatically and took Moe's flame-thrower.

CHAPTER 17

"I'LL NEED SOME MORE GRENADES," groaned Bill, shaking his head at the sheer stupidity of what he was about to do.

"Take my mama's knife," offered Rambette, suddenly all heart. "It's always been real lucky for me."

"This might help, too," said Curly, holding out a box covered with flickering lights.

"What is it?" asked Bill.

"It's a tracking device," said Caine. "I hope. I designed it myself, and Curly built it out of some kitchen utensils and a couple of old transistors."

"How does it work?"

"You press the button like this," explained Curly, leaning over and pushing a green button on the side of the box. "It's set up to respond to all life-forms, but I have a subprogram in it that directs it specifically to okra-smelling life-forms. Right now it's set at maximum range. All these little dots down here are us. That green dot way over there is Barfer."

"What are all *those* dots?" Bill asked.

"Aliens," admitted Caine.

"There sure are a lot of them," said Bill with shivering trepidation. "And most of them are between me and Barfer."

"It can beep, too, if you want," said Curly proudly, quickly moving on. "But there's so many aliens out there it'd be beeping all the time. I'm not sure I like that."

"It's been super nice knowing you, Bill," said Tootsie, giving him a hug. "I just want to tell you I think what you're doing is real noble and unselfish— I feel like crying—even if it is incredibly stupid and probably the last thing you'll ever do. Few things are as beautiful as the love between a boy and his dog."

"You don't want maybe take Slasher, do you?" asked Bruiser. "It maybe slow you down and da aliens would eat you. But I guess I gotta make offer, even if don't much want to."

"That's okay, Bruiser," said Bill. "I guess I ought to travel light and fast."

"You're right about the fast part," said Christianson. "We're kind of anxious to get out of here."

"Take the CB radio, too," said Caine, clipping it to Bill's belt. "That way you can give us good, reliable firsthand descriptions of your close encounters for my report. And if you have any last words, we'll be able to get them down just the way they came out of your dying mouth."

"That's real considerate of you," snarled Bill, checking the fuel level on his flamethrower and wanting to try it out on Caine.

"I'll name my next hybrid okra variety after your memory," said Captain Blight. "*Abelmoschus heroicus billus.* That has a nice ring to it, don't you think?"

"I have to get moving," Bill said, stepping back into the docking tube and firing a couple blasts into the darkness ahead just for good luck.

The anteroom, having taken a good many licks recently, was a pile of smoldering rubble. Parts of dead aliens and ruined spacesuits lay scattered among the scorched debris like joint butts after a party. Most importantly, nothing was moving. Bill adjusted the tracker's range so that he was at one end of the screen and the green dot that was Barfer was at the other. Depressingly, there were far too many alien dots in between.

Bill eased up to the entrance to the main corridor and took a quick and careful peek down the hall. There were too many aliens scrambling around that alley of damnation to count, too many to take out with anything short of a tank loaded with tactical nukes. There had to be another way around.

The air ducts! Bill blessed the unforeseen foresight of the nameless engineer who had designed such handy tunnels so cleverly connecting all parts of the station. He made a pile of broken spacesuits and climbed up to the nearest vent, prying the cover off and pulling himself up with difficulty.

Right away Bill discovered a couple of problems. The air ducts were too damned small and he could barely squeeze through them. Turning around would be impossible once he got started. He now cursed the bowbing engineer who didn't design them a little bigger so a man could sneak around in comfort. There were also no signs to tell him where he was, so he would have to depend on Curly's tracker and his own innate sense of direction to get around. Neither, he realized, was all that dependable.

It was a twisty little maze, and all the side branches

looked alike. Bill pulled himself along in what he hoped was a direction that might be roughly parallel to the main corridor. He had a real depressed feeling from the tracking device that Barfer might be in the alien-infested reactor room. There was nothing to do but keep moving and adjust his position by the dots on the box.

Twice he crawled down blind alleys and had to struggle backwards to the last branch. He decided that if he ever had a chance to design air ducts, not only would he make them large enough to walk comfortably through, he'd make sure they were well lit, clearly marked with road maps, and had an occasional water fountain. The darkness of the tunnels was broken only by the light spilling through the occasional vent, one of which lay directly ahead.

He crept slowly and quietly up to the vent and peered down. The good news was that he was directly over the corridor. The bad news was that there were, if possible, even more screeching loathsome aliens crammed into it than before. Way too many of them were the larger-than-Curly variety who could reach the ceiling vent with no difficulty if they so desired. Bill shuddered at his close proximity to the horrible creatures, and tried to convince himself that they couldn't see him and if he didn't breathe or let his heart beat too loud he'd probably be okay.

"How's it going, Bill?" shrieked the radio at full volume. "Uhuru here."

"Arghh!" whispered Bill, scrambling away from the vent and turning down the volume.

"Are you still alive, Bill? If so, Caine is right here with his notebook, ready for your observations. Got anything to tell him?"

"Tell him he can stuff his notebook!" Bill whispered hoarsely. "This place is crawling with aliens."

"He wants to know if you've got an exact count," said Uhuru. "He says 'crawling' isn't exact enough."

"Look, Uhuru," whispered Bill, pulling himself frantically in what he hoped was the direction of the reactor room. "I'm fighting for my life here. I don't really have time for idle chatter."

"Well, aren't we testy today," sniffed Uhuru. "Then for your information, if you care to know, the ship is almost ready to go. We can wait for you, but not too long. Once we start the countdown, there's no turning back. If you get killed, let us know and we won't bother to wait."

"I'll do that all right," Bill snarled, angrily snapping the radio off.

He hoped none of the aliens had heard the noise. There was no way of turning around to check behind him. The tracker just showed a whole bunch of dots all around him, undoubtedly the aliens in the corridor. At least he hoped that's what they were. He tried to ignore the fact that two of the dots seemed to be following his exact path.

An exhausting and terrifyingly unmeasurable time later, after more twists and turns, Bill was certain they were following him. They must be in the air duct, right behind. And gaining! Bill crawled faster, and in doing so bumped the wall and managed to turn on the beeper function of the box. His heart sank lower with each beep, until it lodged somewhere between his groin and his kneecap, but he didn't dare stop moving long enough to figure out how to turn it off.

The beeps came faster and faster, increasing in volume and frequency with each passing second. He drew his knife, knowing full well there wasn't enough room to use it. The beeps ran together and the dots merged. Something touched his foot.

"Yeow!" yeowed Bill. "Yeow!"

"Keep it down," whispered Rambette. "You want the aliens to know where we are?"

"Rambette!" whispered Bill. "Is that really you? I'm glad to see you even if I can't see you. I can't turn around in here."

"You're not the only one, buster," gasped Rambette. "Bruiser's right behind me. I feel like a slice of ham in a sandwich. On top of that, Bruiser keeps bumping me with Slasher."

"Ain't my fault," sussurated Bruiser. "I'm jammed in like cork."

"Why'd you come?" asked Bill. "This is a suicide mission if I ever saw one."

"Well, let's just say I'm looking after my mama's knife," whispered Rambette. "My heart would break if I lost it."

"I wanna lob more of Uhuru's grenades," snarled Bruiser. "Real great, kill aliens."

"I think Barfer is in the reactor room," whispered Bill.

"We figured as much," muttered Rambette. "Turn right at the next junction. I checked a map of this place before we started out. It's not far."

Bill started crawling again. After he turned right he could see the light of a vent a short distance ahead. When he got there, he looked down. Barfer was at bay in the middle of the room, surrounded by a circle of Curly-sized aliens. Although they stayed a respectable distance from his snapping jaws they writhed and clawed at him. It was only a matter of time before one of them connected. The rest of the ichorencrusted room was thick with creatures slithering and scuttling everywhere.

"Here's the plan," whispered Rambette. "You go on past the vent. I'll take the screen out and jam it in the corner, tying this rope to it. Bruiser and I'll go down first and create a diversion. You follow us and grab the dog. Then we make our escape. Got it?"

"What's a diversion? If mean fight I love diversion," chuckled Bruiser. "Let's go!"

Rambette secured the rope and she and Bruiser slid down it, flamethrowers blasting and grenades flying. As diversions went, this one was right up there in the gold-star range. Aliens were crackling and popping and screaming and flying apart. As Bill slid down, he appreciated the carnage and the fact that Bruiser and Rambette had managed to leave the dog intact.

"Woof!" barked Barfer, plowing through the circle of aliens toward Bill. "Woof, woof!"

"Dey got me!" cried Bruiser, as a slimeball alien wrapped its repulsive arms around him and pushed him into the control board. "Help!"

Barfer sprang into action, leaping on the alien and tearing its throat out.

"Your dog saved my life," cried Bruiser, flopping backwards on the control board as Barfer pulled the alien off him. At that instant an earsplitting alarm bell started ringing. Green lights flashed stroboscopically, bathing the bloodbath with an obscene and ominous flicker. Steam started pouring from the walls.

"What did you do?" cried Rambette, lopping an arm off an alien with her knife. "What happened?"

"I t'ink I fell on da button," admitted Bruiser.

"What kind of a button?" shrieked Bill, gathering up the dog. "What does it say?"

"Hold on," cried Bruiser. "I wipe off da ichor first. Yeah, read it now. It says STATION SELF-DESTRUCT BUTTON. DO NOT PRESS."

"I think we're moving into big problemsville," admitted Rambette. "That button blows the reactor. Move!"

"This station will self-destruct in five minutes," said a bored female voice over the loudspeakers. "All personnel are advised to take necessary precautions. This is a recording. Have a nice day wherever you are and whoever you are."

"Gimme da dog," said Bruiser, taking Barfer and tucking him under his arm, heading for the rope and scampering up it like a monkey. "I makin' tracks!"

Bill followed Rambette up the rope, giving the room five grenades and a final spray on his way up.

As they started scrambling through the air ducts, Bill turned the radio back on and called Uhuru.

"There's been a minor difficulty," he said.

"I've got ears," cried Uhuru, panic in his voice. "There are sirens and buzzers going off everywhere. We're on our final countdown now. I sure hope you make it back in time, because we can't hang around waiting on you."

"Left!" cried Rambette. "Take the next left, Bruiser."

"Why would they have a self-destruct button on a station that costs more than most planets make in a year?" asked Bill, following Rambette like a second skin. "It doesn't make sense."

"It's military," said Rambette. "It's not supposed to make sense. Turn right, Bruiser, right!"

"This station will self-destruct in four minutes," yawned the prerecorded voice over the clanging alarms and the hiss of steam that filled the air.

"Where's all this steam coming from?" cried Bill. "I don't want to be scalded to death after all we've been through."

"I don't know," said Bruiser. "But it sure makes things seem real urgent."

"Turn left!" cried Rambette. "No, wait! Right! All these ducts look alike to me!"

"It's dead end!" howled Bruiser. "We lost!"

"If you care to know, this station will self-destruct in three minutes. Remaining personnel are advised that their chances of survival range from none to zero. Or less. Your only remaining duty is to bend over with your head between your legs and kiss your ass goodbye."

CHAPTER 18

"LET THE DOG GO!" CRIED BILL. "BRUISER! Let him loose!"

"I just got da dog an' you want me to trow him away?" yelled Bruiser. "Get serious."

"I *am* serious," said Bill. "It's a well-known and proven fact that most dogs can find their way back home from anywhere."

"In less than three minutes?" wailed Rambette. "Barfer? No offense, but he's not the brightest dog I've known."

"He's probably hungry," said Bill. "I'll bet he'll head straight for the okra. Put him down and we'll follow him."

"You're betting a lot on a longshot," said Rambette.

"Would you rather sit around and argue about it until the reactor blows? Or maybe you got better ideas?"

"Eaties!" Bruiser shouted as he threw the dog down the duct.

"There he goes," cried Bill as Barfer trotted away. "Follow him!"

The trio scrambled, twisted and crawled after the dog through the dark ducts until—lo and behold—Barfer led them to the vent in the anteroom. They tumbled through the opening and scooted across the pile of ruined rubble to the docking tube.

"Good . . . dog . . ." Bill gasped.

"This station will self-destruct in two minutes. All remaining personnel are advised it is far too late to seek shelter. So have a good day."

"Uhuru?" cried Bill through the radio as they ran up the docking tube. "Uhuru?"

"Sorry, you're too late," he said. "We're lifting off in fifty seconds. Hey, it's been nice knowing you."

"We're at the door," screeched Rambette, grabbing the radio away from Bill. "And we're coming in! If you don't open it, we'll blast it off and you can all suck vacuum when and if you get this crate back into space."

"Well, if you put it like that—" muttered Uhuru, triggering the door latch from the control room.

In a split second, the three Troopers and one dog slid through the opening before it slammed shut with a loud clang.

"Thirty seconds," said Uhuru, as Bill sprinted to the control room.

"Head for da okra room," cried Bruiser, following the dog down the hall. "Dem okra beds is softer den da chairs."

"Me too!" yelled Rambette, passing them in a blur.

"Ten seconds!" said Uhuru as Bill dived into the nearest seat and strapped himself in. "Five!"

"I think maybe I made a mistake in my calculations," wailed Curly. "I don't—"

"Liftoff!" cried Uhuru. "Take it, Curly!"

"We have ignition!" yelled Curly. "Start main engine burn!"

"Our engines are on fire," moaned Tootsie. "We're all going to die!"

"That's normal!" cried Uhuru.

"Dying?" moaned Tootsie. "What's so normal about that?"

"I meant fire in the engines, moron!"

"Glak!!" glakked Curly. "Those G-forces are squishing me to death."

"Better squished than sorry," said Uhuru. "Everybody hold on!"

"Yaw!" cried Larry. "We need a bunch of yaw right now!"

"No, it's pitch we need," interjected Moe. "A whole lot more pitch!"

"You're getting what I give," yelled Curly, punching numbers into the computer. "I'm tired of taking orders from you knuckleheads. Here we go!"

"Watch the shields," cried Uhuru as the ship groaned loudly and the G-forces piled one on top of the other. "Don't overload the shields!"

"Tootsie's right," shrieked Larry. "We're all going to die!"

"Trust me," called Curly. "If we don't get far enough from the station we'll—HOLD ON!—it's blowing!"

The *Bounty* rocked and swayed when it was caught in the subnuclear shock wave as the station and all of its disgusting alien inhabitants were torn apart down to their last ugly, sordid molecule in the raging inferno of the nuclear reactor's self-destruction. It was a good way to go. And go they went until every repulsive hank of orange fur, every last drop of saliva and/or ichor was blasted into nascent atoms.

But it was pretty hairy aboard the ship. The crew swayed left and then right . . . and then left again . . . right . . . blown from side to side like actors in a low-budget movie with a tilting camera. Only this was real-life, heart-stopping action and they screamed and yelled until the ship righted itself and blasted them away from the frightful planet and its appalling inhabitants.

"Let's not do that again," Bill said hoarsely, as they reached orbital velocity and the ship stopped bucking and vibrating. "Are we safe?"

"You betcha!" crowed Curly. "And this calls for a drink!"

"You're on—break out the wine!" cried Tootsie. "We're not going to die after all."

"Go easy on the wine," pleaded Captain Blight, whipping an atomic corkscrew out of his pocket. "It's got to last until Beta Draconis."

"How long will that take?" asked Bill, seizing the corkscrew and stabbing it into the cork on a bottle of white wine. It activated automatically; the cork vaporized in a puff of smoke and the wine bubbled beautifully.

"Probably on the order of two or three months," estimated Curly, holding out a glass for Bill to fill. "That's my best guess. Of course, I could have made a mistake, a grievous error even, and we'll be slogging and trekking through the stars forever. Sorry I said that—but ichor flashback can do that to you."

"Bruiser trust you," that gallant warrior said, leading Barfer into the room. "You done good."

"Gee, thanks," said Curly, blushing and lowering

his head as he held his glass out for a refill. "We all had to do what a man has to do."

"That is a singularly stupid, not to mention male chauvinist pig statement. Pour me," said Rambette, walking into the control room. "Everybody has a glass of wine except Caine, who's the designated android and doesn't count. I want one too."

"And for dis good little dog?" asked Bruiser, holding out Barfer's water bowl. "Fill it to da top."

Bill started to relax for the first time in ages. As he filled the dog's bowl with wine, he felt the pressure sliding from him. After all they'd gone through, it felt good to be safe at last. As tired as he was, he'd probably sleep all the way to Beta Draconis.

"I'm anxious for your report on the mother alien," said Caine. "It's all that's missing from my paper. We really must get it down while it's still fresh in your head."

Bill sank into a chair and shook his head wearily.

"No way. I think you androids are bonkers, around the twist, loopy," he growled. "Or maybe it's scientists I don't understand. While normal people like us, or practically normal, are just trying to stay alive in the middle of the most incredibly repulsive experiences, you're sitting around and asking questions! Go—plant an okra!"

"I can sympathize with your feelings, good shipmate Bill, but someone has to keep the records," Caine demurred. "Otherwise we might not learn from our experiences and the human race would not march triumphantly to the stars."

"What kind of bum-sucking officer-loving creepo are you?" Bill sneered. "Later, maybe—not now. I'm far too pooped to even think about it. Besides that, I think I stink, as do we all, so it's into the recycler shower as soon as this wine bottle is empty."

"Sounds a winner," Uhuru agreed. "But let's kill some more wine first. I'll get another." He had happily shed his spacesuit and garlic necklaces. "White or red? Hey, I think I'll get one of each. Maybe I'll dig us out a snack of tingleberry toasties to go with it."

"You're on," enthused Bill. "We could use a little chow."

"Barfer got away wit'out a scratch," Bruiser said with admiration. "Dis dog's a real scrapper."

"*I* didn't get off that easy," said Rambette, wrapping a bandage around one arm. "We're all lucky just to be alive. I'd rather face an army of Chingers than go another round with one of those aliens."

"They're unhappily extinct now," complained Cain, shaking his head. "Such a loss for science."

"It seems to me you were feeling a little differently when they were climbing up your back," sniffed Tootsie.

"Even androids get inexplicable periods of self-preservation," observed Caine. "Nobody's perfect, though I'm close. However, I realize that in the long run, it would have been vastly preferable for me to have maintained an attitude of scientific objectivity. As it is, the entire repulsive race has perished, and regrettably I haven't even got a single specimen to submit with my paper. Captain Blight has turned all my samples into compost."

"Just this once I agree with the Cap. That's about all they're good for," Tootsie said, raising her wine glass. "Here's to clear sailing and silent running."

"I'll drink to that," said Rambette.

"I'm all for a completely boring and uneventful voyage myself," said Bill. "Nothing but good food and lots to drink and a decent place to sleep."

"That sounds like a house-cat's life—but I agree. And I'm swearing off monsters for life," said Curly, settling back in his chair and adjusting his ear-bandage.

"They're nothing but trouble."

"Something trashed the galley!" cried Uhuru, running into the control room wearing his spacesuit again and three hastily prepared garlic necklaces. "It even wrecked the microwave!"

"What?" asked Christianson. "What happened?"

"It's awful," Uhuru cried. "The galley is ruined. There's ichor and orange fur everywhere!"

"Ichor and fur?" wailed Blight. "Does that mean—"

"It means we're all going to die," moaned Tootsie. "I knew as soon as we got to feeling safe something like this would happen. Is there no end to this madness?"

"I gonna end it now," growled Bruiser, strapping grenades on his belt and grabbing up Slasher. "Hubba-hubba, troopers! All for one an' one for all!"

No one moved.

Bruiser whistled his axe under their noses. "Da way I see it, we got one choice. We get out dere and kill it, or do nuttin' and get et for lunch. Let's go Trojan!"

With great reluctance the crew shuffled out behind Bruiser and Uhuru. They marched to the galley, sticking real close to each other and looking over their shoulders. Never before had the *Bounty* seemed so big, so full of places for alien horrors to hide.

"What a mess," said Tootsie as they stepped into the galley. "It's terrible. There are pots and pans and plates and bowls and skillets scattered everywhere."

"That's just my normal housekeeping routine," said Uhuru. "The damage is back here."

The rear of the galley looked like a bomb had exploded in it. The stove was half-eaten away by alien acid and the door to the freezer had been ripped off. Every surface was covered with ichor and gobbets of fur.

"It got all my steaks," cried Blight, peering into the freezer. "They were prime cuts."

"This way!" Rambette shouted. "I think I've got a trail here."

"Sure looks like it," said Bill, eyeballing the repellent path leading away from the galley. "Uhuru, pass out some more grenades."

"I don't understand how it got in the ship," Uhuru said as he distributed his homemade beauties. "I *know* the ship was clean. I swept it myself with the tracker. And Larry watched the door for every minute after that. Didn't you, Larry?"

"Well, sort of," he said.

"What you mean, *sort of?*" snarled Bruiser. "We risk our lives an' you act like alien doorman."

"I might have dozed off once," he admitted.

"Once?" yelled Uhuru. "Dozed off?"

"Well, it could have been two or three times," said Larry. "No more than five, I'm pretty sure. It was real boring sitting there."

"I'll give you boring!" cried Curly, picking up a flamethrower. "Fry you like an egg!"

"No—please don't! I'm not responsible, it has always been like that. Since I was a child. One moment wide awake—then zonk! All I have to do is close my eyes. I'm able to sleep anywhere, any time. It's a talent I have. I can even do it standing up."

"I'll put you to sleep permanently!" cried Curly. "You let my own personal nightmare back in the ship."

"I can't believe you're related to me," snapped Moe. "If you're my brother, you must have come from another planet, a planet where stupidity is the norm."

"Technically, being clones, you are not brothers," said Caine. "You are genetically identical. A case could be made that you are the same person."

"I'm not buying that," yelled Curly. "That bowby batbrain—"

"Enough sibling rivalry," suggested Rambette. "It looks like it went to Repair Dock Five."

"I hope it's one of the scuttlers," said Blight as they made their cautious way to the repair dock. "That way Bill can stomp it and we're finished."

"I sincerely doubt that we are dealing with a scuttler," said Caine. "The damage in the galley was far too extensive for a scuttler. I would say we have a Curly-sized one on our hands."

"Or maybe even larger," shuddered Tootsie, looking up at the melted door to the repair dock.

"Can we shut up with the wild fantasizing," Rambette ordered. "It ruins morale—which is already pretty low. We'll see what we have when we get there."

The crew climbed through the melted door and looked down into the great expanse of the repair dock. Built to a size to hold a star-class fighter in for dry-dock repairs, it would dwarf anything but the huge alien that stood in the middle of the bay, dripping ichor and handfuls of fur, staring hungrily at them.

"What's that?" cried Caine.

"It's mother," said Bill in a voice filled with sepulchral gloom. "And she just stomped our forklift flat, so we can't pull that trick again."

CHAPTER 19

"WELL, THERE GOES OUR BIG PLAN," sighed Rambette. "I got a feeling that we need a change of strategy."

"We can't kill something that large with our flame-throwers," said Uhuru. "The flames will just smolder the thing's fur."

"Which will make the creature even more angry—if that's possible," moaned Bill. "We've already tried that."

"Grenades? No, dey ain't any better," said Bruiser. "Wotta we do?"

"I'm as close as I'm getting," chattered Tootsie, biting her fist and backing up. "I can't even bear to look at those claws!"

"And while you're not looking don't look at those teeth or jaws, too," said Rambette. "Just when we felt it was safe."

"This is utterly fascinating," said Caine. "Unfortunately for the scientific community, I feel myself slipping into my survival-fear mode and am in danger of losing all my objectivity."

"What are we going to do?" wailed Curly. "This is even worse than my nightmares."

"We could open the cargo doors and blow it out into space," said Larry. "That would work."

"It would," said Bill. "But that would suck us out as well, not to mention draining all the air out of the ship."

"Not the cargo doors—we might be able to get her through the auxiliary airlock," said Rambette. "It'd be a tight squeeze, but it might work."

"It better work!" said Tootsie. "I really like the idea of tossing the alien out into space."

"Sure," said Christianson. "Maybe she'd scrunch in there if we asked her nicely, and stand real still while we closed the inner door."

"Might I suggest that someone could be bait," Caine suggested. "Someone a little tastier than an android could stand in the airlock and look like food."

"We can draw straws to see who's bait," Uhuru said hopefully. "That's a fair way to decide, and I just happen to have some with me."

"No way," said Rambette. "We're in this together, all the way to the bitter end. I say we rush her and with battling courage and superhuman strength back her into the airlock."

"Excuse the expression—but that's incredibly unrealistic. And would probably involve casualties," said Blight. "Maybe even an officer-type casualty." He shuddered at the thought.

"A Trooper's gotta do what a Trooper's gotta do," Bruiser reiterated with simplistic stupidity.

"Maybe we should think it over," muttered Christianson. "I agree with the captain. It might be wisest if we could come up with a plan that doesn't involve possible officerial casualties."

"Too much jawin'!" bellowed Bruiser. "Action. Kill! Destroy! Reenlist! Go! Rambette, you lead. Slasher and me we take up rear—no cowardly stragglers here!"

With great reluctance the herded troops started slowly down the metal steps to the floor of the repair dock. As they reached the halfway point, the alien charged them. Larry threw all his grenades at once as Rambette and Bill opened fire with their flamethrowers. The alien staggered back just long enough for the crew to finish their scramble down the steps.

"We split two teams," yelled Bruiser. "Force dat t'ing to da airlock."

"I'm not being on Larry's team," cried Moe.

"How about three teams?" Curly suggested ingratiatingly. "I vote for three teams and personally volunteer to go back and watch the door."

"We ain't got time to count ballots," cried Rambette. "You! You, you, and you come with me. Over this way! Now! The rest of you go with Bruiser."

Bruiser yelled, "Get over here!"

"He's beginning to sound worse than an officer," complained Larry as he shouldered his flamethrower and lined up beside Tootsie. "He's ugly enough to be one, too."

"Back her up easy. Dose of you wit da flamethrowers, use 'em. Go! Go! Go!"

The flamethrowers roared into action, bathing the giant monster with a wall of flame. Uhuru hurled grenades at the thing's feet, keeping her hopping around, but otherwise doing no noticeable damage. Bill felt like his finger was welded to the FULL POWER button on his makeshift flamethrower.

"Spread out!" cried Rambette. "You stand that close together she'll take you all out with—*hey!*— watch that tail!"

Rambette's team scattered as the mother alien swung her massive tail in a wide arc, catching Captain Blight in his massive stomach and sending him flying and bouncing across the floor.

"My leg!" he cried. "It's broken!"

"Then shoot sitting down," yelled Christianson, dodging another swing of the tail and throwing two grenades. "Don't be such a coward, Blight. It's only a leg."

"Hold your fire!" cried Rambette. "Back off! She's got Caine!"

The smoldering beast held Caine in her enormous clawed hand, jaws dripping ichor as her huge teeth clacked horribly mere inches from the android's face. The smell of smoldering orange fur was singularly revolting.

"I'll get him!" cried Larry, dropping his flame-thrower and running past a stunned Rambette, grabbing two knives from her belt and leaping at the monster.

He landed on the creature's kneecap and was climbing up a furry leg, hacking and slicing away, when she reached down and plucked him off, holding him at arm's length. The indescribably repulsive alien looked hungrily first at Larry and then at Caine.

"Come on, Curly!" cried Moe, running toward the monster. "We've got to help Larry!"

"I'm right behind you!" called Curly. "You take the right leg. I've got the left!"

In an instant the mother alien was crawling with clones. Her initial reaction was to bite off Caine's left hand. She grimaced and spit it out, throwing the android down and turning her attention to the presumably tastier trio of cloned humans.

Bill rushed to Caine and dragged him away from the action.

"It'll be okay," lied Bill, tearing his shirt and wrapping it as a tourniquet around the android's severed arm. "Try to stay calm."

"I am losing considerable hydraulic fluid," moaned Caine, his eyes fluttering. "Please tighten the tourniquet. I must doze now, my batteries are so weak. . . . If you could locate my missing appendage, there is the faintest possibility it could be reattached."

"I'll get it," said Bill.

"I'm . . . drifting away . . ." whispered Caine. "Thank you for your assistance. Good luck. And, maybe, goodbye . . ."

The android closed his eyes. He lay still and stopped breathing. Bill wondered if he was dead. Or had he ever been alive—at least in the strictest sense—to begin with? He tried to remember what he knew about android physiology and drew a big fat blank. He put his ear to Caine's chest and heard gears grinding and relays snapping on and off. At least the android was still running.

"Here's his hand, Bill," said Tootsie, laying the chewed-on extremity gently on Caine's still chest. "You've done all you can for now. We'd better go. Bruiser needs help."

Bruiser and Rambette had gone on a clone-rescuing mission. Bruiser was hacking at one leg with Slasher while Rambette gave the creature a flamethrower hotfoot on the other. Uhuru was astride the wildly swinging tail, sawing away at it with one of Rambette's biggest pig-stickers.

"She's going to eat Larry," cried Curly, who had

a precarious grip on one slippery shoulder.

"I've got it!" Moe yelled, scrambling up the alien's rib cage like it was a ladder. "Take this, you alien mother!" he screamed as he tossed a grenade between the creature's gnashing jaws.

It was one of Uhuru's finest grenades and went off with a tremendous roar. The alien dropped Larry and staggered back with smoke puffing from its ears. Curly fell off, but Moe somehow managed to hold on.

"What did it do?" cried Bill, helping Rambette in her attempt to fry the foot. "Did you kill her?"

"I think it might have chipped a tooth," moaned Moe, peering into her horrible mouth. "I'm abandoning ship!" he cried, jumping down.

Barfer was circling the alien, growling and snarling in a really convincing imitation of a ferocious dog, snapping at any handy part that came near.

"I'm all busted up," cried Larry. "I can't walk!"

"Dis is *it!*" snarled Bruiser, taking a full-force swing with his axe, finally breaking through the alien's thick skin. What passed for alien blood spewed out as the creature fell to one knee.

"Splatter that punk!" roared Tootsie, spraying the nearest arm with Larry's flamethrower.

"Watch out!" cried Uhuru. "She's falling over!"

Everyone scattered as the massive mother fell to the floor, still snapping her fearsome jaws and grabbing at anyone within reach, dripping ichor and blood, crawling and snarling.

"Everyone here!" cried Bruiser. "Gotta force her back into da airlock."

It was a toss-up as to who was doing the forcing. Even with all the remaining crew providing a solid front, flamethrowers and grenades were just about even with claws and fangs. It was two crawls forward and one crawl back. Bill's flamethrower ran out of fuel and he used it for a club until the alien batted it away. Then he turned to lobbing grenades. At last they had the creature backed up against the open outer door to the airlock.

"What now?" cried Tootsie. "She's not going in!"

"Me and Slasher gonna convince her," growled Bruiser.

The big man went face-to-face against the sprawled-out monster, swinging his axe at anything within axe-length. Alien fingers and toes went flying. Barfer had a death-grip on the tip of her tail. Bruiser hacked and chopped. The creature retreated back into the airlock, but not before she lashed out with one bleeding arm and sent Bruiser skidding across the floor into the flattened remains of the forklift.

"Hey! Dat t'ing broke my arm!" he roared. "Close da door and dump her!"

"It won't close!" moaned Curly, pressing the green button. "The switch is broken!"

"Let me at it," yelled Tootsie. "I'm the queen of the switches!"

She tore the cover plate off the wall and dug into the switch's innards with a knife. One of the alien's hands reached out and grabbed her tightly around the waist. Tootsie fought desperately as Rambette hacked at the creature's gigantic hand. Sparks flew from the switch and the door started to close.

"Back off!" cried Uhuru. "Get away!"

"Help!" yelled Tootsie, using all her strength to keep a claw from spearing her. The door stopped, jammed against the alien's arm. It was all that kept the airlock door from closing.

Bill charged to the door.

"I can't hardly breathe!" gasped Tootsie. "I'm going to die!"

"Not yet," said Bill, leaping into the air and landing on the arm with his elephant foot. The weight of it pushed the arm down and back. The door slid shut with a sharp clang.

Rambette hit the red button and a loud whooshing sound vibrated the walls as the outer door opened and the air pressure blew the alien out into deep space.

The crew sat stunned. It was over.

Blight moaned. Bruiser staggered over and picked up Slasher with his good arm.

They were battered, broken, and bruised. But they had won.

"You did good—for a MP, Bill," said Bruiser.

"We all did good." Rambette started gathering up her knives. "It was a group effort. Even Christianson carried his own weight."

"I rather enjoyed the tossing grenades part," he said. "They ought to teach that in officer's school."

"Where's Caine?" asked Rambette. "I lost track of him."

"He's over there," said Bill. "Right next to the— *No! No! It can't be!*"

"Now I'm *sure* we're going to die!" cried Tootsie as an alien even larger than the mother monster came snarling and dripping slime out of the shadowy back corner of the repair dock.

"Over there!" cried Curly. "There's another one! There are two of them!"

"Three!" yelled Christianson as another alien

lurched into sight. "And each one is bigger than the one before."

"I think I agree with Tootsie," said Bill. "This time we're all going to die."

CHAPTER 20

"I HAVE A RATHER IMPORTANT OBSER-
vation to make," said Caine, sitting up, looking down
gloomily at the severed hand in his hand.

"We don't need observations," sighed Rambette.
"What we need is an instant miracle."

"It was naive of us to assume that this colony had
but a single mother," said Caine, speaking with some
difficulty. "Single-parent families are the norm only
in the most primitive of species."

"So we got both mothers and fathers breathing
down our necks," said Rambette. "Big bowby deal.
Our flamethrowers are empty. We're almost out of
grenades. We're crunched and beat to death, got broken arms and legs. And you want to discuss family
ways?"

"No," gasped Caine, a LOW HYDRAULIC
FLUID light flashing on his forehead. "What I wanted
to discuss was a highly relevant observation."

"Observe away," said Bill. "We're goners any way

you cut it. I figure we've got about thirty seconds
before they make up their minds to charge."

"Who among us has not been attacked by the
aliens?" asked Caine.

"We've all been attacked and crunched," said Tootsie. "None of us are immune, not even you."

"No, wait!" said Bill. "Barfer's been left alone.
They seem to avoid the dog."

"Maybe it's his breath," moaned Tootsie. "Pass
out the dog biscuits."

"That's close," said Caine, his LOW BATTERY
light glowing brighter. "What does the dog's diet
consist of?"

"Okra," cried Bill. "He won't eat anything else."

"And where is the one place in the ship we haven't
seen any aliens?" asked Caine.

"The control room?" guessed Curly.

"No, I saw them there once," said Uhuru. "Guess
again, and guess quickly. I think they're getting ready
to eat us."

"The okra room!" cried Bill. "There's never been
one in the okra room."

"Clear thinking," suggested Caine, his LIFE
FORCE DRAINING light blinking weakly. "I
strongly suggest that we retire to the okra room and
bar the door. However, someone will have to carry
me. I no longer have sufficient hydraulic fluid remaining to enable my legs to function."

"You mean we might have a chance?" said Rambette.

"Only if we hurry," said Uhuru, lifting Caine.
"They're coming."

"I got some signal flares," said Curly. "Okay to
throw them?"

"Why not?" said Bill, taking one and tossing it. "Everybody close your eyes!"

The room was filled with a powerful bright light, and the aliens staggered around, confused and temporarily blinded.

"Leave me a flamethrower," said Captain Blight, crawling forward. "I'll keep them occupied while you escape."

"Are you serious?" asked Bill.

"Not really," said Blight, "but I thought I ought to make the offer before I asked someone to carry me out. My broken leg, you know."

"Around dis way," cried Bruiser. "Den up da stairs."

They went as fast as they could, which was not very fast on account of all the people that needed to be carried and their various wounds and bruises. With incredible weariness they reached the stairs, just a few steps ahead of the snarling aliens.

"Here go the last of the flares," said Curly, throwing them in front of the ichorous monsters.

It was a temporary measure, but it bought them just enough time to make it to the top of the stairs, then out the melted door before the aliens recovered. They set a new world record in the wounded troopers-running-down-the-corridor-to-escape-from-ichorous-aliens category, handicapped division. Finally they reached the okra room and piled inside, bolting the heavy steel door in place and stacking bags of potting soil in front of it. Only then did they turn their attention to repairing their various injuries.

"How much oil he take?" asked Bruiser, his arm in a sling made out of plant stakes.

"He's down three quarts," said Bill, checking Caine's dipstick. "I think he'll come around after his batteries have time to recharge."

"It was brave of you guys to come after me," Larry said to Moe and Curly. "Of course, I would have done the same if our positions had been reversed."

"Sure, knucklehead," said Moe. "I guess maybe you would."

"I wish we hadn't tossed the mother alien out the airlock," mused Blight, leaning on a rake he was using as a cane. "She would have made wonderful compost."

"You want to try for one of the others?" asked Tootsie. "There are three potential compost heaps out there just wandering around drooling ichor and shedding fur waiting for you to hit them on the head with your rake."

"Ten," said Uhuru shaking his head. "I got the tracker back. It shows ten huge aliens and about a hundred smaller dots that are probably pods, or maybe scuttlers. Most of the aliens are right outside the door."

"I, for one, am not planning any strolls in the near future," said Christianson. "This looks like a good place to ride out the voyage."

"We may not have that choice," said Bill, standing by the door and holding his hand against the metal. "This is starting to heat up. I think they're using acid on the other side."

"But the okra—" said Tootsie.

"They're so hungry, I bet they would eat anything," said Bill.

"True," said Caine, sitting up and blinking his eyes. "And if they're laying eggs, they'll need even more food. We can assume—*hey!*—what happened to my hand?"

"Good job, huh? Bill and I put it back on," said Curly proudly.

"It's upside-down," cried Caine. "You did it wrong!"

"It's the only way it would fit," said Bill. "Some of the wires had been chewed on pretty badly and wouldn't reach the other way."

"This is awful," moaned Tootsie. "What are we going to do?"

"We could try splicing some more wires," said Caine, examining his hand and flexing it. "We could probably get it going that way."

"I figure we've got a half-hour before they get through the door," said Rambette. "If anyone has a plan, it better be a quick one."

"We could press the ship's self-destruct button," said Curly. "There's one in the control room."

"Wonderful. You're a moron," said Bill disgustedly. "That would blow us up, too, bowb-brain. I'm all in favor of not bringing any of the aliens back, but I do have my limits and you bumped into one of them right there."

"How about if we blow the air valves on the rest of the ship but leave this room sealed off?" asked Uhuru. "Suck all the air out. Could that be done?"

"It's possible," muttered Blight thoughtfully. "When I designed this room I made it as independent as it could be. It has its own air and water systems. The door and the two air vents that connect with the rest of the ship will need to be sealed, but that's all."

"I can weld the door shut!" shouted Bill. "But how are we going to blow the air from the rest of the ship?"

"A few well-placed bombs ought to do it," said Uhuru, grinning. "I'll blast the *Bounty* so full of holes it'll look like Swiss cheese."

"I can patch the autopilot into the garden computer," said Curly. "We can run the ship from here."

"A *garden* computer?" asked Tootsie. "That little thing over there by the flower pots?"

"If it can run an irrigation system, I can make it run the navigation system, warning controls, navigation feedback parameter loops, and atomic engines," said Curly. "The principles are roughly the same."

"I advise haste," Caine said hastily. "Time is of the essence."

Things started hopping. Blight and Caine mixed gunpowder while Christianson helped Uhuru construct the bombs. Bill went to work creating an airtight seam around the edges of the door with a heavy-duty electric welder. Tootsie devised a clever magnetic clamp to hold the explosives in place. Moe made several timing devices out of a pile of rusting garden equipment and assured everyone the bombs would go off simultaneously. Rambette volunteered to go through the air ducts with Uhuru and help him put the bombs where they would do the most damage.

"Remember, we don't want to blow the ship apart," said Blight, helping Uhuru into the air duct. "We just want to poke a few holes in it. Don't get carried away."

"Let's do it," said Uhuru, hauling up a bag of bombs.

"In spite of everything, and despite the mutiny, I feel that I *am* responsible for this ship," said Blight. "If it is destroyed, they'll take it out of my pay. I can afford a few holes, but total destruction is beyond my budget."

"If it's destroyed, you won't be around to worry about it," said Rambette, following Uhuru.

"Now that's a cheerful thought," said Blight, turning to Bill. "How is the welding going?"

"Not bad," he said, bending over the torch. "If you would move that extension cord for me, I could reach the far corner."

Things were scuttling and scratching just on the other side of the door. Bill could all too easily imagine the mob of aliens gathered there, scant inches from where he stood. He drove them from his mind and finished the door, moving to the air vent that Uhuru and Rambette weren't using.

Caine had come up with steel plates to cover the vents, and he and Blight held one in place while Bill tacked the corners down. Then he started sealing the edge.

"Something's coming!" cried Tootsie.

"What do you expect?" said Christianson. "There's a whole gaggle of aliens outside the door."

"No," she moaned. "There's something coming through the air duct Uhuru and Rambette went into."

"It's too early for them to be coming back," said Curly. "Far too early."

"It's getting closer!" moaned Tootsie. "I can hear its rasping breath!"

"Wow!" cried Curly. "Here it comes!"

Bill turned to the other vent and thumbed his welder to maximum flame. Only the fact that his extension cord was too short prevented him from frying Barfer when he came bounding out of the duct, closely followed by Bruiser.

"You scared the life out of me," moaned Tootsie. "Where have you been?"

"I had ta get back to my bunk. Got some t'ings dere," said Bruiser sheepishly.

"What things?" cried Curly. "What could possibly be so important you'd go out there and risk your life against all those aliens?"

"I left dis pitcher dere," he said. "It's da only one I got of her."

"You must really love your mother," said Bill lachrymosely, shutting off the welder.

"Mother?" cried Bruiser. "I never had no mother. I was government issued. Dis my girlfriend's pitcher."

Bill took the picture Bruiser held out for him. The woman looked like a female Bruiser, a sumo-wrestler-sized mountain of muscle.

"She's—hideously attractive," said Bill, handing Bruiser back the picture. "And I can tell there's a lot of her to love."

"T'anks," said Bruiser. "And I found dis under your bunk." He handed Bill a fair-sized box and a folded piece of paper.

Bill took the box, opened the paper and read it.

Dear Bill,

If you live to find this, it may be of some possible use to you. I hope you won't take offense but that foot of yours is about the ugliest thing I've ever seen, and certainly can't be comfortable to schlep around. I have taken the liberty of providing you with the means of replacement. Simply press the red button to start it up, and when the green light comes on, stick that repulsive appendage of yours in the hole. The resulting bud should take about two months to grow out.

Your Chinger friend,
Eager Beager

P.S. Don't forget our little agreement. Keep up the good work spreading dissension in the ranks.

"What is it?" asked Bruiser.

"Didn't you read it?" Bill asked, crumpling the note into a small ball and putting it in his pocket.

"Don't read too good," said Bruiser. "Like books wit lotsa pitchers."

"It's a package from home," lied Bill.

"Cookies," grunted Bruiser, taking the welding torch from Bill. "Hate cookies. Here, I'll finish dat."

"I'm sure that you will all be excited to know that I have completed the first draft of my scientific *tour de force*," said Caine, holding out a fifty-page tome held together with an oversized paper clip. "It will take me some time to finish it, since I have to share the computer with the autopilot, and typing with an upside-down hand is rather difficult."

"Here we come!" yelled Uhuru, as he and Rambette came tumbling out of the vent. Blight and Christianson immediately slammed the steel plate in place and Bruiser started welding.

"It was terrible!" Uhuru cried. "Horrible!"

"Did the aliens chase you?" asked Curly "Did they almost catch you?"

"No," said Uhuru. "But going through those ducts was awful. They're too small—and dark? There is no darkness like the darkness in an air duct. You can't turn around in them and it's easy to get lost. It's a stupid way to travel if you ask me. I ripped my spacesuit, too. I have galloping claustrophobia and hay fever—*Achoo!*—from all the dust in there."

"Forty-five seconds," said Moe. "The charges are about to blow. Are you finished with that last seal, Bruiser?"

"Yeah," he said. "*Hey!*—da flame's out! Da room's dark!" A feeble emergency light came on.

"We blew a fuse!" cried Tootsie. "There's no way to stop the bombs. We're going to lose all our air and die!"

"Give me that report, Caine!" shouted Bill.

"This is no time for research," said Caine as Bill grabbed it away from him, pulling off the paper clip and throwing the papers away. "Hey ! My paper clip!" Caine shouted. "It's the last one on the ship!"

Bill sprinted across the room and ripped open the fuse box, jamming the paper clip across the main terminals.

"Five seconds!" cried Moe as the lights flicked back on and Bruiser's torch lit. "Three."

"Got it!" cried Bruiser as the ship shook violently, tossing them left . . . then right . . . then left again.

"Are we . . . ?" asked Larry.

"Did it . . . ?" asked Moe.

"Can we . . . ?" asked Curly.

"We're okay," sighed Rambette. "I heard a lot of swooshing and crashing and some noises that sounded exactly like aliens getting sucked through the hull into outer space."

"Let's eat!" cried Curly. "Where's that food, Larry?"

"What food?" he said. "You were supposed to get the food."

"Don't look at me," said Moe. "I was busy making the timers for the bombs."

"What are we going to do?" moaned Tootsie. "We finally get rid of the aliens, and now we're going to starve to death." ·

"Not quite," sighed Bill. "I think Barfer has the right idea."

The dog was standing in the middle of an okra bed, wagging his tail. He had a few choice sprouts in his happy mouth.

Three weeks later Bill pressed the red button and got rid of his elephant foot. He figured after all this time, it was safe to abandon his stomper. The resulting bud was little and pink, but there was no telling what it might grow out to be.   ·

Everybody was totally revolted by okra, even though Captain Blight had shown remarkable imagination in devising new ways to prepare it. He could do everything with the plant except hide the fact that it was okra. Curly's best estimate was that it would be another six to eight weeks before they could expect the opportunity to change their diet.

The day after Bill stuck his foot in the hole, he thought he saw something scuttle between two of the okra beds. He hoped it was a mouse, but he had a funny feeling it wasn't.